PRAISE FOR

INSERT COIN TO CONTINUE

"*Ready Player One* for the middle grade crowd. . . .
A winning pick that's ideal for gamers or reluctant readers."
–School Library Journal

"[An] enjoyable adventure with plenty of laugh-out-loud moments."
–Bulletin for the Center of Children's Books

"A fun and easy read for students who have always wondered
what it would be like to live in their favorite video game–or for
students who are just trying to survive a day at school."
–School Library Connection

"An entertaining romp."
–Publishers Weekly

JOHN DAVID ANDERSON

ALADDIN
New York London Toronto Sydney New Delhi

FOR FUN

ALADDIN

An imprint of Simon & Schuster Children's Publishing Division
1230 Avenue of the Americas, New York, New York 10020
First Aladdin paperback edition September 2017
Text copyright © 2016 by John David Anderson
Cover illustration copyright © 2016 by Orlando Arocena
Also available in an Aladdin hardcover edition.
All rights reserved, including the right of reproduction in whole or in part in any form.
ALADDIN and related logo are registered trademarks of Simon & Schuster, Inc.
For information about special discounts for bulk purchases, please contact
Simon & Schuster Special Sales at 1-866-506-1949 or business@simonandschuster.com.
The Simon & Schuster Speakers Bureau can bring authors to your live event.
For more information or to book an event contact the Simon & Schuster Speakers Bureau
at 1-866-248-3049 or visit our website at www.simonspeakers.com.
Cover designed by Karin Paprocki
Interior designed by Mike Rosamilia
The text of this book was set in Avenir LT Std.
Manufactured in the United States of America 0817 OFF
2 4 6 8 10 9 7 5 3 1
The Library of Congress has cataloged the hardcover edition as follows:
Names: Anderson, John David, 1975- author.
Title: Insert coin to continue / by John David Anderson.
Description: New York, New York : Aladdin, [2016] | Summary: Middle-schooler Bryan
wakes up to find that his life has become a video game, with bullies to beat, races to run,
puzzles to solve, and much more at stake.
Identifiers: LCCN 2016021972 | ISBN 9781481447041 (hc) | ISBN 9781481447065 (eBook)
Subjects: | CYAC: Video games—Fiction. | Middle schools—Fiction. | Schools—Fiction. |
Bullying—Fiction. | BISAC: JUVENILE FICTION / Boys & Men. |
JUVENILE FICTION / Sports & Recreation / Games. | JUVENILE FICTION / Social Issues / Bullying.
Classification: LCC PZ7.A53678 In 2016 | DDC [Fic]—dc23
LC record available at https://lccn.loc.gov/2016021972
ISBN 9781481447058 (pbk)

CONTENTS

PROLOGUE:
DEFEATING THE DEMON KING ...
AGAIN

"Greetings, chosen one. I have been expect-ing you."

"Yeah, yeah. Let's just get this over with."

"Pass me the chips, will ya?" Oz asked.

Bryan shook his head. "Not your waiter, man. Or your mom."

"I had hoped you would join me, but now I see that your heart is impure. I have no choice but to—"

"Destroy me, yes. Got it."

Oz stuffed his face. "His voice sounds like that guy from the movie previews. Movie preview guy. *I have no choice but to destroy you! Bwa-ha-ha!"*

"You sound nothing like that guy."

"You sound nothing like that guy. Bwa-ha-ha!" Oz repeated, trying to sound even more like that guy and failing.

"Just keep eating and be quiet. Here comes the big speech, all about how I journeyed through the twelve gates and drank the dragon's blood, on and on and on." Bryan started clicking. "'Do you choose to confront the Demon King?' Oh, heck yeah." Bryan clicked yes.

"Then let us begin, warrior, so I can wallow in a bath of your cruor."

"What's cruor?" Oz wanted to know.

"I think it means guts and stuff."

"This is so awesome."

"I know, right?"

On the screen the Demon King raised his bloody ax and started attacking. Bryan clicked much more frantically.

"You should have totally used your Potion of Alacrity," Oz chided.

"Nah. I've already got Lord Romlor's Blessing of Infinite Graces cast on me; it wouldn't do any good."

JOHN DAVID ANDERSON

"Dude, he's summoning zombies."

"Got it, thanks."

"Oh man, Lightning Fists. See how they glow like that? Quadruple damage."

"I am looking at the same screen you are, Oz."

"Whatever. Watch out for that pit. And those spiky boulder things. Really, you equipped your Mace of Flaming Vengeance over the Vorpal Blade of Bloodletting?"

"The Sovereign of Darkness has a weakness to fire."

"I *did not* know that." Oz was impressed. It didn't take much.

"That's 'cause you've never gotten this far. And try to chew with your mouth closed. You're dribbling."

Oz brushed the crumbs from his shirt onto the carpet.

"Now we just switch to the Rod of Annihilation to bring down his force field like so. . . . Then hit him with a level-fifty death incantation wrapped in a big burrito of spiritual wrath. . . . Stab him through the heart for good measure and . . . voilà. The Demon King is toast."

"*NOOOOOOOOOOOOOOOO!!!*"

"Dude. You disintegrated him."

"I know."

"*[Cough, cough, cough] . . . You have acted bravely, hero. Your quest is complete.*"

"That's it?"

"That's it."

"What a loser."

"Total lamoid. Okay. Here's the part I keep telling you about. See just back there, right behind the credits. Right . . . *there.* Do you see it?" Bryan paused the screen and pointed.

"No."

"You don't see it?"

"What am I looking at?"

"That tiny little flashing spot there in the corner that looks sort of like a key?"

"That chunk of the burning dark lord you just exploded?"

"No, that one. Right . . . there."

Bryan Biggins moved his cursor to the speck in question, then spun around in his chair and looked at his best friend. "I think that's it. That's the thing that unlocks the secret bonus level. But I don't know how to get it. I've tried everything. Checked all the guides. Read all the posts. Nobody's found a way."

JOHN DAVID ANDERSON

"You mean the secret bonus level that doesn't exist," Oz said.

"Say what you will. I know it's there. These guys put one at the end of all their games."

Oswaldo Guzman licked his fingers, then wiped them on Bryan's bedspread. "I don't know, dude. Maybe that little flashy speck is just something they put there to tease pathetic dweebs like us that have nothing better to do on a Saturday night than sit around a computer and play the same game all the way through for—what does this make for you—the eighth time?"

"Ninth."

"Right. See? *That's* what I'm talking about." Oz fell back on Bryan's bed and stared up at his ceiling. "So dweeby."

"I'm telling you it exists. I'm going to find it. I'm going to unlock it. And I'm going to beat it."

Oz looked in the bag of barbecue chips to confirm it was empty, then let it fall to the floor. "And even if you do, then what?"

Bryan picked up the empty bag, crumpled it, and tossed it on the overflowing metal trash bin under his desk. He didn't know "then what." He hadn't really thought about "then what." The point was beating the game. Completing the quest. Figuring out the secret. There really was no other reward. Was there?

"I don't know," Bryan said. "I'll just . . . win, you know? *Winning?* Perhaps you've heard of it."

Oz shook his head. "I've *heard* of it. Listen, do you think maybe we could take a break from video games and watch a movie or something? I'm starting to go cross-eyed." Oz rolled off the bed and onto the floor, landing with a grunt. Bryan stared at the computer, where Sovereign of Darkness finished its theme music, zooming in on the remains of its title villain, now just a pixilated puddle on the screen.

The Demon King's reign of madness had ended. The credits rolled. For the ninth time.

But Bryan didn't think it was over. He didn't *want* it to be over. He still felt like he was missing something. He stared at the mysterious little flash in the background for a second more and then shut down the computer.

He couldn't begin to guess what came next.

THURSDAY
THE DAY BEFORE FRIDAY

BLEEP. BLEEP. BLEEP. BLEEP.

Bryan swept out blindly and missed the alarm clock, floundering for the snooze button before finally shutting it up. He pulled himself up in bed and stared through the open slats of his blinds. It was still dark outside.

That was the worst part about school days. Having to get up before the sun. That and the school part.

Outside, he knew, the leaves had turned, spray-painting branches in bursts of orange and red, con-trasted with the emerald carpet of manicured lawns, but this early all he could see were shadows. Bryan stretched and stumbled toward the bathroom, dodging towers of laundry, trying to muster some enthusiasm. It was a Thursday, which at least made it close to Friday. That was something. He could hear his mother banging around in the fridge downstairs. She would already be in her tracksuit, drinking a vitamin shake and watching The TODAY Show. She had a crush on Matt Lauer. Bryan's dad didn't seem to mind.

Face washed, teeth brushed, he slipped back into his room and into cleaner-at-least clothes, glancing at his computer, where the title screen for Sovereign of Darkness stared back at him. He had played another couple of hours last night, foregoing his desire for a good night's sleep in the hopes of uncovering the secret bonus level that he was sure existed.

He hadn't found it.

Maybe Oz was right. Maybe it wasn't there. But Bryan had a problem letting things go. It wasn't determination, exactly. He had given up on lots of things over the course of his life—soccer, piano lessons (he still played the saxophone at least), karate, a perfect complexion, an A in math—but occasionally he would fixate on something, let it nag him, like an itch on the roof of his mouth. Finding the secret bonus level to Sovereign of Darkness was one of those things.

On-screen, Kerran Nightstalker—the character Bryan had nursed from level one to level fifty through a steady diet of Mountain Dew–driven demon-bashing—spun his sword and stared heroically, as if he had spotted a pack of imps on the horizon and was begging Bryan to sit down and give him orders. *Come on, Bryan*, the dark elf whispered. *Play ten more minutes.* But Bryan couldn't be late for school. Not again. He grabbed his backpack and hurried downstairs.

Bryan Biggins was a level-fifty, dual-wielding dark elf ranger only some of the time. The rest of the time he was a freckle-cheeked boy, short for his age, living at the end of a cul-de-sac in a neighborhood known for its high rate of community garage sales, and attending a school known for its unwritten uniform of North Face jackets and Hollister jeans. A place where everything looked the same from a distance. It was disconcerting sometimes, the sameness. The identical mailboxes. The columns of minivans ranging in hue from slate gray to charcoal gray. The flat-topped hedges marking the boundaries between copycat houses. Sometimes it was hard to tell anything apart.

Bryan checked his reflection in the mirror above his dresser; he looked nothing like Kerran Nightstalker. He was scrawnier, for one, and his eyes were blue, not green. His nose rounded into a knob at the end, as if it were always slightly pressed against a window. Bryan didn't own a flaming mace, though the crop of orange curls on his head sometimes gave the appearance that his skull was on fire. He had never held a sword in his life and had never slain anything, unless you counted the caterpillar he had accidentally rolled over with his Big Wheel when he was five. His mother said he cried for almost an hour.

And unlike Kerran Nightstalker, Bryan had never been in a fight. He had been pushed. Shouldered. Tripped. But he'd never taken a punch. He was no adventurer. Some days he didn't even feel like the main character in his own life.

"Bryan, you better hurry. You're going to be late!"

Bryan came down the stairs and snatched a waffle from the freezer. His mother handed him a glass of milk. "You're not even going to toast that?"

"Nope," Bryan said, cramming half of the ice-crystal-crusted waffle in his mouth.

"You were up late again playing that stupid game, weren't you?"

"Mrff wrff frrm frrfrrwr." He swallowed his milk in three gulps and went in for the hug. "Don't want to be late," he reminded her. She tried to sneak in a kiss, but he dodged it. Mom kisses were totally uncalled for.

"Have a good day," she called out after him.

He said he would, but he really doubted it.

Bryan pedaled hard, still chewing his frozen waffle. It was a two-mile ride to school, which some mornings felt like the Tour de France, but it was still better than taking the bus. On buses nearly anything was fair game, as long as it could be done in secret behind the sticky vinyl seats and out of sight of the driver. On the bus in elementary school, Bryan had once been forced to mash a banana in his armpit—actually peeling it and sticking it underneath his shirt and squeezing—and then eat the sweaty remains. So when he finally graduated to middle school, he begged his parents to let him bike. To his surprise, they agreed. They didn't know about the banana-armpit incident, but they had heard other horror stories. Plus, like all parents, they insisted that exercise was good for you.

Bryan arrived at Mount Comfort Middle School with sweaty but bananaless pits and five minutes to spare. He chained his bike and sped through the halls to his locker, where Oz was dutifully waiting and shaking his head.

"Almost late again."

"I know," Bryan said.

Bryan had lots of friends—at least fifty or so online, half of whom he recognized and at least ten that he could remember having spoken to in real life. Mostly, though, Bryan had Oz: the self-proclaimed Wizard of Elmhurst Park and unconfirmed holder of the world record for Pixy Stix slamming (twenty-three in one minute) and the only kid at Mount Comfort who looked up to Bryan. Oz was second generation. His parents had come to the country from Puerto Rico, packing little Oswaldo in Mrs. Guzman's belly, only two months from delivery, ensuring he would be 100 percent American when he arrived.

Oz was born to be a magician. You don't name a kid Flash and then not expect him to try out for football. Or name your daughter Moonbeam and then act surprised when she pierces her nose. And since there were no such things as wizards—not in real life—magician seemed the next-best thing. Oz had a whole trunk full of magic paraphernalia in his closet: top hats and disappearing coin boxes, weighted dice, little red balls, and an array of colorful scarves. Strangely, having a trunk full of silk scarves didn't up his cool factor any at school.

Bryan couldn't endure life at Mount Comfort Middle School without him, though. They had been best friends since they were six years old and both of them peed on Mrs. Bucherwald's maple tree together. It didn't matter to Bryan that Oz was always too loud and a little overweight. It didn't matter to Oz that Bryan had pasty vampire skin and seldom wore matching clothes. They had marked their territory, and that was enough.

"Okay, so I was watching episode fourteen of *The Firelight Chronicles* again last night, and I think I know who's behind the Enigma Virus," Oz began breathlessly.

"No you don't," Bryan said, opening his locker and finding his books. *The Firelight Chronicles* was a show he and Oz watched that featured space pirates, aliens, androids, and female actresses dressed in black leather. Bryan was pretty sure he and Oz were the target audience. "They're not going to tell you who's behind it. They *want* you to speculate."

"It's Dr. Raznor," Oz continued.

"Too obvious," Bryan said.

"Which is why it *is* Dr. Raznor." Oz nodded, winking. "Because they know that you know that it's obvious, so they know that you know that it's not him, which means it *has* to be him."

Bryan rolled his eyes and fished out his math book. He had math first period. Who in their right mind decided that dividing fractions was best done at eight in the morning?

"Let me guess. You were too busy playing SOD to watch. Did you get any closer to finding the secret level?"

"Not for lack of trying," Bryan said, digging through the discarded candy wrappers for his social studies notebook—the one he should probably have been studying last night. "I'll try again tonight, provided Old Man Jenkins doesn't overload us with reading."

Jenkins was Bryan's social studies teacher. He was

only in his early forties, but he already had gray hair and his breath smelled of butterscotch. He was better than Fossil Frieda, the senile art teacher who refused to retire and croaked like a frog from too many years of smoking. She insisted that Lady Gaga was the name of a French Impressionist painter and worried that Elvis Presley was still a corrupting influence on America's youth. She had probably never even played a video game in her life.

"I think you're wasting your time," Oz said matter-of-factly.

Bryan looked at his friend, eyebrow cocked. "*Excuse* me? Playing the same game over and over again in order to unlock a secret level that may or may not exist is *not* a waste of time," he countered. "Besides, do I even need to remind you of the time you spent sixteen straight hours playing Super Plumber Seven? At least I didn't leave my butt print permanently engraved on the couch in my basement."

"I was in the zone," Oz protested. "And you can't even tell it's my butt. And that's not the point. The point is . . ."

Oz didn't say what the point was. His voice trailed

off. He pointed behind Bryan. "Girl," he whispered. "And she's coming straight for us." Oz looked down at his feet. Bryan turned around.

It wasn't just a girl. Or not just *any* girl. It was Jess.

"Oh. Hey," Bryan said, suddenly conscious of what the bike ride had done to his hair. It probably looked like a giant orange starfish had suckered to his skull and then died there. He tried to smooth it down, all casual like. He only made it worse.

"Hi, Bryan. Hey, Oz," Jess said.

"Uh. Um. Wuhuh?" Oz said, using the vocabulary he reserved for all female encounters. Not that Bryan blamed him. This was Jessica Alcorn. Just Jess to anyone who knew her. The same Jess that Bryan had sat next to in third grade. The one he wasn't allowed to talk about anymore because Oz had gotten tired of hearing about her. She stood an inch taller than both of them and had what Bryan's mother would call an olive complexion, though it looked nothing like any olives he had ever seen, closer to the color of a walnut. Today her black hair splayed out over her shoulders and stretched to her elbows. Her long legs were tucked into knee-high black leather boots. She wore a white patterned sweater that reminded him of snowflakes. But mostly it was her eyes that struck him. Chocolate-hued with flecks of orange. Like late autumn. Bryan blinked twice.

"I'm not interrupting, am I?" Jess asked, tucking her hair behind her ear the way all girls somehow learn to do. Bryan cleared his throat.

"No. Um. Actually, I was just telling Oz about this video ga—" Bryan stopped himself before diving headlong into total, hopeless nerddom. "I mean, I was just headed to class," he amended.

Oz nodded dumbly. "Headed to class," he repeated.

"Oh," Jess said, adjusting her backpack, "because I wanted to ask you if you had anything going on tomorrow night. Missy Middleton is having one of her little get-togethers at her place."

Jess paused. Oz licked his lips. Bryan stared. He had never been to Missy Middleton's house. He had never gotten so much as a casual wave from Missy Middleton, let alone an invitation to come over.

"Sooo . . . ," Jess continued, stretching the word like taffy, "she said I could invite whoever I wanted."

Bryan put a hand on his locker door. His tongue felt

like a sponge left out in the sun. He tried to stay calm, taking a deep breath without *looking* like he was taking a deep breath. He felt Oz scoot next to him so that their shoulders were touching, as if he were trying to attach himself permanently, like conjoined twins.

"Practice," Bryan heard himself blurt out. Beside him, Oz grunted. Jess cocked her head. "Baseball practice. Like, all night. Sorry."

"I didn't know you played baseball," Jess said.

"Yeah," Oz said through gritted teeth. "I didn't know you played baseball."

"Right. Just started. This year," Bryan said sheepishly.

Jess smiled. It was her polite smile, not her real one. Bryan knew the difference. He had all her facial expressions cataloged, knew when she was angry or annoyed or upset or proud of herself. He'd been watching her for years.

"It's all right," she said. She didn't sound disappointed, exactly, which was disappointing. "Well, if practice gets canceled and you change your mind, here's Missy's address." She held out a scrap of paper filled with her hurried handwriting. Bryan took it, and for a very brief moment their fingertips *almost* touched.

Oz turned and punched Bryan in the shoulder after Jess walked away. "*Baseball* practice?"

"What did you want me to say?"

"Oh. I don't know. How about, 'Um, yeah, we'll be there'? I mean, is that so hard? The girl you can barely shut up about just asked you out!"

"She didn't ask me out," Bryan mumbled. "She invited *us*—me *and* you—along with probably a hundred other people, to a party where, undoubtedly, *we* would get stuck in a corner wishing we were somewhere else, while *she* hung around with someone much cooler. Besides, if you wanted to go so badly, why didn't *you* say something?"

"You know I can't talk to women," Oz said.

"You can talk to Myra."

"Myra doesn't count."

Bryan sort of knew what he meant. Myra Felton was their lunch buddy and sometime gaming companion. A friend first and a girl only as an afterthought, though Bryan was pretty sure she secretly (and somewhat inexplicably) had a crush on Oz. Oz didn't know this, of course. He sometimes had trouble figuring out which shoe went on which foot, so expecting him to pick up on the little flirty cues Myra dropped was asking way too much. "Besides, Friday night's game night," Bryan reminded him.

"Every night is game night," Oz said, almost making it sound like a bad thing. He glanced at his watch. "Whatever. We really are going to be late now." Oz grabbed his backpack and looked Bryan straight in the eyes. "Seriously, though. Reconsider. You can still cancel your imaginary baseball practice. I haven't been to a party in over a decade."

"You're only twelve."

"I know. Think about it." Oz put a finger to his skull, then turned and disappeared into the crowd—the one magic act he was actually good at. Bryan looked down the hall to see Jess talking with some of her girlfriends.

Oz was right. He should have just said yes. He wasn't sure why he didn't. After all, this was the same girl who had sat at his table in the third grade and shown him how to make a second layer of skin out of Elmer's glue, peeling it off in strips so they could examine the prints. The same girl who had personally given him a special valentine with one of those little candy hearts. The same Jess who last year had asked if she could borrow his lip balm during a field trip to the planetarium, not even wiping it off before handing it back. They had known each other for nearly five years. They'd been in the same reading groups. They'd bounced in the same bounce houses. They'd once gone to the same party at the Roller Cave and accidentally run into each other, Jess offering to help him up and Bryan refusing, afraid he'd just drag her down.

For over a third of Bryan's life, Jess had been there, like a satellite, hovering around him, just out of reach. They smiled and waved and had three-sentence-long conversations, and then he watched her from a distance, wondering if he would ever have the guts to tell her just how often he thought about her, wondering if she ever thought about him.

Unfortunately, she was also the same girl who had recently been seen hanging out with someone else. And not just anyone. The star of the Mount Comfort Middle School basketball team and unanimously voted God's gift to the universe, Landon Prince. Perfect golden crown of hair. Teeth so white they had to be bleached. Eye-traceable stomach muscles. Landon had been seen walking Jess home several times already this year, which is all it takes to make the whispers start. And those whispers were what Bryan had heard in the back of his head when Jess asked him if he was free this Friday.

He stood by his locker and watched her laughing with her friends. If this were the movies, she would turn and look his way. She and Bryan would lock eyes for a second or two, and then she would bite her lip (that way girls do) and turn back around and he would know he'd made a serious mistake turning her down.

But this wasn't the movies.

Bryan watched her vanish around the corner without a second glance. There were no do-overs. He had blown it. He sullenly reached into his locker for his copy of *Romeo and Juliet*, when a familiar voice made him freeze.

"Bilbo Biggins."

Bryan felt his stomach clench. He turned to get a look, just to be sure, though there was no mistaking the voice.

"Hi, Tank," Bryan said, thinking of burying himself in his locker like a snail retreating into its shell, but Christopher "Tank" Wattly slammed it shut before he had a chance. Tank Wattly resembled a white rhinoceros and had a neck like a tree trunk, on which sat his oversize, block-shaped head. He was dressed, as usual, in his letter jacket and combat boots straight out of the Second World War. He towered easily over Bryan.

"How's life in the Shire?"

It was an old joke, one that Bryan had endured since the second grade. It came with the last name. Bryan doubted Tank had ever even seen any of the *Lord of the Rings* movies, let alone read the books. He some days doubted Wattly could read at all.

Bryan put his hands in his pockets and took a step back instinctively, trying to decide if there was any way to play this so that he could avoid getting picked on. This wasn't his first encounter with Wattly. If he could just navigate the conversation without saying anything offensive, he would probably sneak by with just a little more name-calling and a mild shoulder shove.

"Just trying to avoid the big, ugly Orcs," Bryan said.

Mission failure.

"What'd you just call me?" Tank said, suddenly closing the already-too-short distance between them.

"No. Not you . . . I mean, just, because of your

comment about the Shire . . ." Bryan tried to backtrack, but it was too late. The kid whose friends had nicknamed him Tank for his ability just to roll over opposing linemen on the football field pushed Bryan up against the lockers with one hand, pinning him there like a human Post-it note. Bryan could count the brown hairs on Wattly's knuckles. He looked around for a teacher. Or the principal. Or anyone with a stun gun and the authority to use it.

"Listen, Tank . . . ," Bryan said, his breathing getting harder. "Let's be honest. Beating me up isn't going to make you feel any better about yourself."

"Are you suggesting I should feel *bad* about myself?" Tank asked, his face reddening.

Bryan tried to squirm free, thinking of how much easier life would be if he really were a level-fifty dark elf ranger like Kerran Nightstalker. He would just summon a swarm of flesh-eating locusts to go to town on Chris Wattly, leaving nothing but bones. As it was, all Bryan could do was kick his legs and hope the bell rang soon. Several kids had turned around to watch, giving Wattly an audience, which made things even worse. Tank pressed harder and Bryan felt like his ribs were about to crack.

JOHN DAVID ANDERSON

"C'mon, Wattly, just let him go."

Suddenly the pressure on Bryan's chest lifted and he dropped to his feet. Wattly stepped back with an angry flash in his eyes. Bryan took a deep breath and straightened out his shirt and then turned to see his savior, thinking maybe it was Mr. Vincent, the assistant principal, or one of the other teachers. But it wasn't. It was Prince. Maybe the only kid in the whole school whom Tank didn't look down on.

"Tank" and "Prince." And he was stuck with "Bilbo." Life was beyond unfair sometimes.

Wattly looked over at Landon Prince, then back at Bryan. His giant, strawberry face was all crumpled up, as if he were trying to add two-digit numbers. Finally he took one of his meaty hands and brushed imaginary dust off of Bryan's shoulder. "Tell Frodo I said 'hi.'"

"Will do," Bryan said, then gave Tank a two-fingered salute. All the kids who had been watching turned away, losing interest now that there was no potential for bloodshed. Not that there would have been a fight, exactly, just a one-sided pummeling. Bryan watched Tank lumber down the hall, passing close by Landon, who didn't even flinch.

"You all right?" Landon asked. Mouth full of pearls. Hair perfectly coifed. Bryan almost thought he saw a halo, too, but that must have been the reflection of the halogen lights above.

"Yeah, I'm fine," Bryan said, reaching down and picking up his bag so as not to make too much eye contact. Tank made Bryan feel weak, but Landon Prince just made him feel small.

"Don't let Chris get to you; he's got anger management issues. You sure you're okay?"

Bryan Biggins finally looked up into that handsome face. Yes. Life was completely unfair and the universe was a callous, good-for-nothing jerk.

"Yeah," he said. "Whatever. It's no big deal." He couldn't bring himself to say "thanks," even though he knew he should. He couldn't say it because Landon Prince didn't need it. Bryan didn't get to be the center of the good-for-nothing-jerk universe. Not like Landon Prince. Bryan wasn't the one the girls whispered about at lunch. Or the one the teachers beamed with pride over. He wasn't the one who got to walk Jess Alcorn home.

The universe had thanked Landon Prince plenty already.

The bell for first period rang. Bryan was late. His math teacher, Mr. Tennenbaum, would probably write him up. Figures. First Jess, then Wattly, and now this. He had been at school less than fifteen minutes and already was having a terrible day.

He should have just stayed at home and smashed imps.

It didn't get any better. The disapproving look from Mr. Tennenbaum when Bryan came in late—the warning not to let it happen again. The tanked social studies quiz—to be expected due to the total lack of studying. The fact that it was turkey and noodles at lunch. Oz spending half the day bugging him about Jess's party. The bugging, the bullying, the Shakespeare, the quizzes, the walking through the halls with your eyes on your shoes so that nobody noticed you, the fact that nobody noticed you—after all of it, the last bell finally rang, and Bryan felt like he had just been released from purgatory. He headed to his locker and met up with Oz, who promised he'd try to come over if his mom let him. Bryan nodded and headed for the door, hoping, at least, that his bike hadn't been stolen.

And that's when he saw her. Or saw them, rather. Her sitting on the ledge edging the stairs to the school's front entrance. Him hovering over her. Bryan just stood at the door and watched, jostled by all the other kids scrambling for their buses. Landon Prince had a hand on her shoulder. Her hands were on her knees, legs crossed. He must have said something funny, because Jess laughed a little, then smiled. Her real smile, not the one she'd given Bryan that morning.

Someone shouldered Bryan out of the way from behind, causing his backpack to slip off and tumble down, spilling its contents across three stairs. Someone else kicked his math book and it skidded into the street, forcing Bryan to go after it. By the time he had gathered everything up, Landon and Jess were gone.

That night after dinner, homework, and a forced hour of family time where he and his parents did the dishes and then played a game of Clue (Bryan wanted to guess Tank Wattly in the hall with his bare hands, though it was really Mrs. Peacock with the candlestick in the study), Bryan sat behind his closed bedroom door and called Oz to tell him about what he'd seen after school. On-screen, Kerran Nightstalker was torching his way through a horde of goblins on his way to the Demon's Lair. For the tenth time.

"So he walked her home. Big deal. I'd let you walk me home."

"I don't want to walk you home," Bryan said.

"What? I'm not good enough for you anymore? You're lucky to have me."

Bryan snorted, not wanting to admit that Oz was right. "It's not just that, though. The whole day was horrible. It's like no matter what I do, I can't win."

"You feel like your life is on hard-core mode," Oz mused.

"Something like that."

"Everybody's life is on hard-core mode."

"So sayeth the wise Oswaldo."

"I'm just saying, everybody feels that way, like everyone else is out to get them. Everybody feels like their life is the worst and that nobody understands."

"I doubt Landon Prince feels that way."

"Whatever, dude. I'm not the one that turned Jessica Alcorn down today. It's not like you didn't have your chance."

He was right about that, too. Oz was seldom right about two things in a row. It was disconcerting.

"You think we should have said yes."

"I think *you* should have said yes," Oz replied. Bryan could hear Mrs. Guzman's voice yelling in the background. Oz's mom had a distinctive voice—distinctive, meaning loud enough to wake the dead. "Listen, I gotta go. I'll see you tomorrow, all right? Friday. Game night. That is, unless you have baseball."

"Game night," Bryan repeated.

Bryan hung up and then finished off the last of the goblin guards outside the Demon King's temple. The music ratcheted up, synthesizers bleating in a minor key.

"Greetings, chosen one. I have been expecting you."

He couldn't fault Jess for choosing Landon Prince. Trouble was, he couldn't hate him for it either, no matter how much he wanted to. Just that morning Prince had kept Bryan from having his heart ripped out of his chest *Temple of Doom* style. There was no competition where Bryan could possibly triumph over Landon Prince. Except maybe video games. And Bryan couldn't imagine a world where winning a video game earned you the heart of some girl you'd been crushing on since the third grade.

"Then let us begin, warrior, so I can wallow in a bath of your cruor."

He should just let it go. She probably had no idea that he thought about her constantly, that he kept that same thing of lip balm hidden in his dresser next to that third-grade valentine, the letters on the candy heart almost smudged out of existence. She had no idea because he never bothered to tell her. He could barely get a word out when they did talk, let alone say how he really felt. He didn't have the guts. It was useless even thinking about it. Bryan stabbed the Demon King through his own black heart and watched him explode.

"NOOOOOOOOOOOOOOOO!!!"

He stared blankly at the screen, having forgotten why he was even doing all of this again. The music swelled. In just a moment the credits would roll, and Bryan would be right back where he started. He began to push away from his desk, when the theme music to Sovereign of Darkness suddenly, inexplicably, cut out.

Bryan paused, then pulled his chair up to the desk with both hands. He watched as the pixilated remains of the Demon King slowly reassembled themselves, piece by piece, from clawed feet to horny crown, until he was completely re-formed.

This had never happened before.

Bryan hitched a breath, his skin tingling, chest tightening. The Demon King knelt down in the center of the screen, holding his giant sword before him in deference.

"Congratulations, warrior. It is time for your true journey to begin."

"Shut. Up." Bryan reached for his phone, finger poised over one of only three numbers in his speed dial. Then, suddenly, the screen flashed black, then green, then black again. All black. Entirely black.

The game was gone. Everything was gone. Sovereign of Darkness had closed. Shut down. Bryan was just staring at a blank black screen.

"Oh no. No, no, no, no, no, no, no, no." He clicked the mouse. Left. Then right. Scrolled. Pressed the space bar. Return. Escape. A bunch of random keys. Pounding. Clacking. Nothing. Blank screen. "What? What did I do? Where did you go? Come back!"

A line of neon-blue text appeared at the bottom of the screen.

INPUT ERROR.

"What the heck?" Bryan hit the enter key several times rapidly.

JOHN DAVID ANDERSON

INPUT ERROR.

INPUT ERROR.

INPUT ERROR.

INPUT ERROR.

He pressed Ctrl+Alt+Delete. A new blue line appeared.

TRANSFER PROTOCOL FAILURE AT XP1. USER RECONFIGURATION REQUIRED. REINITIALIZING.

That didn't sound good. "Reinitializing? Reinitializing what? What are you doing, you stupid machine?" Bryan pounded on the top of the monitor with his fist.

The screen suddenly erupted with text, marching left to right, flooding from the bottom up. Bryan caught only traces of words he recognized: "download," "host," "corrupted." Lots of numbers. Enormous strings mixed with symbols, like a cartoon character's curses. This wasn't good at all. He was sure he had somehow infected his computer with a drive-crashing virus. He reached down for the power switch, ready just to kill it, his elation at having *maybe* unlocked the hidden level of the best game of all time replaced with dread at having to tell his parents that he had ruined the $800 desktop they had gotten him for his birthday. He reached down to the box, which was radiating heat like a furnace, its fan in overdrive.

Then he stopped.

The text had come to an abrupt halt, leaving only one line flashing, this one at the top of the screen.

PRESS ANY KEY TO CONTINUE.

Bryan took a deep breath. He sat up in his chair.

PRESS ANY KEY TO CONTINUE.

He reached out and hesitantly tapped the space bar.

ARE YOU SURE (Y/N)?

"Am I sure?"

Bryan couldn't remember the last time he was 100 percent certain of anything.

He knew what he should do. He should just unplug the thing and give it a minute to cool down and then restart. He should leave it alone. Odds were nothing good could come of this. Nothing at all.

Then again, if he continued . . .

Bryan held his breath and pressed the space bar.

There was a sound, a soft whimper like a metallic sigh, and then the whole thing shut down. The computer. The monitor. The speakers. All of it. As if it had blown a fuse. None of the buttons were flashing. The fan stopped its steady whir. Dead. He'd killed it.

Bryan cursed and banged on the keyboard a few times, then counted to ten and pressed the power button on the tower. Nothing. The monitor wouldn't even come on. The whole thing was fried.

"Terrific! Just terrific!" He kicked at the computer and it rocked back and forth. His parents were going to be so ticked. Bryan crawled under the desk, checked the plugs, jiggled the wires. No effect.

He looked at the clock. It was 11:37. He had school tomorrow. His mom would hissy fit big-time if she knew he was still awake. He listened for her footsteps in the hall, afraid that his own cursing had woken her, but there was only silence.

There was nothing he could do about it tonight. He would have to deal with the broken computer tomorrow after school. Maybe he could take it over to Mike Merano's. Mikey was a big math geek who sometimes rebuilt computers and phones and stuff in his garage. Maybe it had just blown a circuit. He tried one last time to power it up, saying a short prayer, but to no avail. Then he collapsed onto his bed without even pulling up the sheets and buried his face in a pillow.

INSERT COIN TO CONTINUE

That had been it. The secret level. He was sure of it. And then the whole thing had come crashing down. As usual.

Oz would never believe him. Nobody would. With his computer fried there was no telling what damage had been done. His saved games were probably gone. The software could have been corrupted. Still, *he* knew. He had been right on the cusp of something magical.

It is time for your true journey to begin.

He couldn't worry about it. Tomorrow was Friday. He would have the weekend to mess with it. Maybe he could get the computer fixed, reload the program, get his character back to the level it was. It would take hours. Days. But he could at least get started. He had the whole weekend to himself.

It wasn't as if he had anything better to do.

FRIDAY, 7:00 a.m.
THE FIRST COIN

↓

BLEEP. BLEEP. BLEEP. BLEEP. BLEEP. BLEEP. BLEEP. *Bleep.*

Bryan swept out blindly with his hand and missed. It took three more attempts before he managed to silence the alarm.

He didn't move. He still felt exhausted, drained. It couldn't be morning already. He had been deeply immersed in this dream where he was battling a giant gorilla on the roof of a hotel. The gorilla was throwing humongous fruit at him—oversize apples, rolling oranges—and Bryan had to leap, ballet style, over each one as it came barreling toward him. The trouble was, he kept running and jumping but he wasn't getting anywhere. He could see the end, but he couldn't reach it. The alarm pulled him out of the dream just as he was tumbling over the ledge.

The dream must have worn him out, the sheer thought of running and jumping for his life. His legs were still asleep. He couldn't get them to move. Bryan pulled himself up on his elbows and rubbed his eyes, afraid to get to his feet until he got some blood back into them, knowing they would crackle as if the nerves were on fire. He looked over at his alarm clock to confirm what time it was.

The clock read 7:01.

In itself unpleasant, as always, but that wasn't all. This morning there was another message.

INSERT COIN TO CONTINUE.

Bryan shoved his fists into his eyes again, then blinked repeatedly, staring at the words written above the clock in iridescent blue. Just hanging there above Bryan's nightstand like a holographic projection. Bryan reached over to touch the letters, but as soon as his hand went through them, they vanished.

When he brought his hand back, they reappeared.

INSERT COIN TO CONTINUE.

"I'm still asleep," he murmured. He shook his head, trying to lose the image of the strange electric-blue words hanging above his clock, and went to swing his legs out of bed, hoping a shower would wake him up. He was delirious. He could use some caffeine. Maybe he could steal some of his father's coffee.

His legs didn't move.

They *wouldn't* move. They were two solid blocks under his camouflage bedspread. He could see their outline in the blanket, could even *sense* them, muscle and bone. His brain sent out the signals—*Come on now, legs, get moving, up and at 'em*—but they wouldn't obey.

He was paralyzed from the waist down.

Bryan started to panic. He pounded on both legs with his fists, willing them to wake up. He was about to call out for his parents when a thought occurred to him.

Maybe he *hadn't* woken up yet. Maybe this was still just part of his dream. In a couple of minutes his real alarm would go off and he would be back in his normal bedroom with his normal legs, which would move like normal legs do. Bryan closed his eyes and kept them closed for a moment. When he opened them again, he noticed something flashing beside him. The words above the clock had started blinking on and off.

INSERT COIN TO CONTINUE.

INSERT COIN TO CONTINUE.

INSERT COIN TO CONTINUE.

And beneath them, now, was a number.

20, it said. Then, **19, 18, 17.** And with each second the message would flash.

INSERT COIN TO CONTINUE.

16. 15. 14.

Bryan pinched his arm, hard enough to make himself wince, then glanced down at the alarm clock. There was a slot in the center of it that he was certain hadn't been there before. Just above the snooze button. The kind you might find in the top of a piggy bank. Just large enough for a quarter.

INSERT COIN TO CONTINUE.

12. 11. 10.

Next to the clock lay the contents of Bryan's jeans pockets, emptied the night before. His phone. A mostly empty pack of gum and eighty-eight cents in change.

JOHN DAVID ANDERSON

INSERT COIN TO CONTINUE.

8. 7.

Figuring that it was still part of his dream somehow and disoriented by the numbers counting down, Bryan grabbed a quarter from the pile and dropped it in the slot on the clock. He heard it hit metal, clinking its way along, as if it were traveling through some steel-walled labyrinth before settling somewhere seemingly far away. Instantly the timer stopped and the words disappeared.

Bryan could feel his legs again.

They were just fine. Completely responsive. He slid out of bed, gingerly testing his footing. "Okaaaaay," he whispered to the empty room. He looked at the alarm clock. No words. No slots. Just 7:02.

He walked to the bathroom, putting a hand against the wall to steady himself. He needed that shower. Priority one. He took a good look at himself in the mirror while the water warmed. His eyes were bloodshot. He was several weeks overdue for a haircut. Otherwise, he looked normal. Tired but normal. Bryan took a deep breath and stepped into the tub, letting the steam envelop him.

When he emerged, he felt better. More like himself. He wandered back to his room and looked at the alarm clock again. Still just an alarm clock. Maybe he had just imagined the whole thing. Some kind of after-sleep delusion. He dug in the pile of laundry by his bed for yesterday's jeans and put them on, then slipped into a blue-and-white T-shirt that didn't smell too bad. He pocketed the stuff on his nightstand, put on his socks and tennis shoes, and checked himself in the mirror.

He held his breath. There stood his reflection, looking back at him in his old blue jeans and ratty shirt. Except listed along the sides of his profile, suspended in midair again, were those same pixilated blue letters. This time they didn't say anything about inserting a coin. Instead they were labels that pointed to Bryan's outfit.

There was an arrow pointing to his jeans.

BREECHES OF ENDURING STIFFNESS. +1 DEFENSE. COLD RESISTANCE +10%.

And another pointing to his shirt.

TUNIC OF UNWASHING. +1 DEFENSE. -2 CHARISMA.

One pointing to his shoes.

BOOTS OF AVERAGE WALKING SPEED. FIRE RESISTANCE +5%.

And pointing to his head was still another arrow. Next to it was the word **NONE**.

Bryan looked behind him to see if the words were projected on the opposite wall somehow, but they could only be seen in the mirror. He looked down at his shoes. Three-year-old Adidas cross-trainers that he'd had long enough to buy new laces for. "Boots of Average Walking Speed?" he repeated to himself. He glanced back at the mirror, reading the labels silently, then quickly looked around the room and found his Chicago Cubs baseball cap dangling from his bed-post. He reached over and grabbed it, then stood back in front of the mirror and put it on.

Where the arrow pointing to his head had once said **NONE**, it now said: **HELMET OF ENDURING FAITH. -1 INTELLIGENCE. +5 PIETY.**

He took the cap off, back on, off, back on. The words changed accordingly, appearing and disappearing with every move.

"Okay. Now I'm just going crazy," he muttered to himself.

From downstairs he heard his mother call him. He quickly stuffed his books into his backpack and slung it over his shoulder, taking one last glance in the mirror and freezing there.

BURDENSOME BAG OF KNOWLEDGE, the mirror told him, pointing to his pack.

"Definitely crazy," he repeated, then headed for the stairs.

His father had already left for work. Professor Biggins had an 8:00 a.m. class on early American history, teaching college kids why grown men wearing powdered wigs should be considered heroes. His mother was fighting with the toaster, trying to pry out a bagel that it had swallowed whole and wouldn't let go of. Bryan glanced in the hallway mirror, but the words didn't appear again. Maybe he had just imagined them, too.

"Mom, do you notice anything . . . different about me today?"

Bryan looked around the kitchen, making sure nothing else was flashing, counting down, asking him for money. Everything looked normal. His mother afforded him a quick once-over.

"You need a haircut," she said. Then she returned to her battle, turning the toaster upside down and shaking it.

"No. I mean anything . . . strange. Like blue writing or flashing lights or anything."

She turned and stared at him, the half-burned bagel in one hand, the toaster in the other. She suddenly looked distressed. Beyond burned-bagel distressed. "You're not sick, are you?"

"I don't know. Do I look sick?" He didn't *feel* sick. He just felt . . . disoriented. He wished he hadn't said anything. His mother was the type A of the family. Prone to panic. She threw the maligned bagel into the trash, then came up behind him and put her wrist to his forehead. "You don't feel warm. Were you up late again last night?"

He didn't see the point in lying to her. Of course, he didn't see the point in telling the whole truth, either. That's just how you handled your parents. "Yeah, a little."

"Well, maybe if you eat something, you'll feel better." She handed him an untoasted bagel—at least it wasn't frozen—and a glass of orange juice. He finished the juice in four swallows. Then nearly dropped the glass, his hands suddenly shaking. Flashing in front of him, so quickly that he barely had time to register it, was another message.

+1 FORTITUDE.

He looked down at his empty glass, then over to his mother.

"Did you just see that?"

"Did I see what, dear?"

It was gone. There was nothing for Bryan to point to. She stared at him, clearly concerned again. In a moment she would be taking his temperature and then hauling him off to the MinuteClinic. That sounded like even less fun than school.

"Nothing," he said, then looked at the clock on the microwave. Somehow it was already 7:39. "I'm going to be late again." He stuffed his bagel in the front pocket of his Burdensome Bag of Knowledge and moved toward the door.

"Listen. I won't be home until late tonight, so you and Dad are on your own for dinner."

Bryan nodded distractedly, kicking the door open with a Boot of Average Walking Speed.

"But call me if you feel like something's wrong, like if you get sick or something. I'll come and get you."

If he felt like something was wrong.

"I'm fine, Ma," he said as he left, letting the screen door bang closed behind him. But that was just to keep her from worrying. It wasn't even *close* to the truth.

Something was *definitely* wrong.

7:42 a.m.
NEED FOR TEN-SPEED

RIDING OUT OF HIS NEIGHBORHOOD AND ONTO THE main road that would take him to school, Bryan considered his morning so far. The little blue messages. The numbers. The slot in the alarm clock.

Insert coin to continue. He had heard that phrase before, though he had never actually *seen* it anywhere. Not until this morning. His father had told him about growing up spending his Saturdays in video game arcades, standing in front of boxes taller than him with stupid names like Dig Dug and Galaga—long before kids carried a hundred games in their hip pockets.

Back when arcade-style games cost only a quarter, gas cost a dollar, and people wrote letters in something called cursive, mailed with something called stamps. Of course, none of that explained why Bryan had had to put a quarter into his alarm clock just to get out of bed this morning.

Maybe he really was just imagining things. Yesterday had been rough. He had a lot on his mind. A little hallucination wasn't completely out of the ordinary, was it? His mother always said he had a big imagination. And his great-grandmother used to see things all the time—fairies, angels, UFOs—except according to everyone else in the family, she was completely off her rocker. Or it could be hormones. According to the "life skills" coaches that had come to their school at the start of the year, hormones messed with the brain of every kid in middle school, leading to countless psychological changes and considerably more armpit hair. Surely they could be to blame for a little morning craziness. And hadn't he spied his very first chest hair just yesterday? And the zit on his shoulder? It was all chemical.

Bryan almost had himself convinced when a man

on a bike passed him on the left, dressed in one of those form-hugging blue suits with yellow stripes and a neon-blue helmet to match. As he passed, Bryan thought he saw the biker pump his fist, as if passing a twelve-year-old kid meandering his way to school was some real accomplishment. Bryan realized he was pedaling awfully slowly, lost in thought, and quickened his pace. He didn't want to be late for school again. Certainly not for math.

Another biker came up on Bryan's left, moving just as quickly as the first, dressed like a cardinal in flame-red Lycra, her hair flapping behind her, her eyes masked by sunglasses. As she passed, she actually bumped Bryan a little, her legs brushing up against his, knocking him off balance. He swerved out into the road for a split second before righting himself.

"Hey, watch it!" Bryan shouted. He wasn't prone to shouting at adults, but the woman had nearly bowled him over. He had been biking this route for weeks now and never had a problem before. In fact, he seldom ever saw any other bikers on the road at this hour, and now there were two. Bryan looked behind him.

There were so many more than two.

JOHN DAVID ANDERSON

There were at least a dozen more bikers behind him, coming up quickly. Somehow Bryan had found himself in the middle of a high-speed race down Mount Comfort Road. He looked toward the sidewalk, thinking of just getting out of the way and letting the other bikers pass, but the sidewalk was narrow, less than half the size of the bike lane, and every other driveway held a parked car blocking the way. He could stop and let everyone pass, but he was already late.

So instead he started pedaling faster, legs churning, trying to stay ahead of the rest of the pack. He glanced behind him again. The flock of riders was gaining. They all wore helmets and sunglasses, looking eerily similar in their synthetic suits, like a posse of neon-clad, bicycle-riding CIA agents determined to hunt him down. In a matter of seconds they were on him. One passed on the left and quickly cut in front of Bryan, making him veer right into the curb, his backpack shifting, nearly causing him to topple over again. He made a quick adjustment and got back on course as two others passed him on either side, bent over their handlebars, focused only on the path ahead.

"Seriously, people!" Bryan shouted. But either they

couldn't hear him or they were ignoring him. In fact, the two that had just passed him sideswiped each other, colliding, it seemed, on purpose. Their front wheels crashed, handlebars seeming to tangle, before they finally pulled away, one of them hopping the curb and plowing into a mailbox, raising his fist in anger. Bryan considered stopping to make sure the rider was all right, when he felt something bump him from behind.

He turned to see a large man barely contained in a clingy red-and-blue suit, looking like an overweight Spider-Man, nudging Bryan's back tire with his front. The man had a mustache that stretched beyond the perimeter of his cheeks, curling up at the ends. He was holding on to the handlebar with one hand. The other was holding a banana. An actual banana. He nosed into Bryan's back side again, causing him to teeter.

"What the heck?" Bryan screamed at him, waving. "Go around! Go around!"

As if the idea hadn't occurred to him, the man with the sinister-looking mustache swerved left and changed gears, accelerating past Bryan, who inched right to make room. Up ahead he could see the turnoff for the school parking lot, right next to the baseball diamond. More bikers continued to pass him on both sides, riding recklessly, leaning into one another, forcing one another off the bike path and onto the curb or out into the street. Bryan saw one of them spin out of control and go down, but he just as quickly brushed himself off and remounted. Another biker skidded in front of him, causing a spray of muddy water to kick up into Bryan's eyes. He bent his head down to his shirtsleeve to wipe his eyes, afraid to let go of the handlebars with either hand. He blinked rapidly, clearing his vision, then looked back up.

Mustache man's head was turned. He was smiling. In his hand he held the now-empty banana peel.

Bryan watched it fly through the air. Saw it hit the ground right in front of him. Felt a strange sensation as his front tire caught it, the bike's handles twisting, everything sliding out from beneath him, his stomach somersaulting as he veered hard right into the school parking lot, desperately trying to keep control. The bike toppled sideways and crashed hard, it and its rider coming to a skidding halt on pavement still damp from the previous night's rain.

Bryan cursed and looked back at the column of

riders, who raced on, careening wildly down the street. He gingerly inspected his elbows and knees, the former only slightly scraped up, the latter protected by his Breeches of Enduring Stiffness. His bike helmet had protected his head. His palms had bits of loose gravel pressed into them. His bike seemed to be in one piece still, though its front wheel was twisted a full 180 degrees, and there was half a banana peel woven into its spokes.

But the scrapes on his elbows and the damage to his bike were nothing compared with the thing he was looking at.

There, in the blacktop of the parking lot, itself a web of cracks and fissures, was a perfectly rectangular slot about an inch long. And hanging above the slot, suspended in midair, were familiar blue words.

INSERT COIN TO CONTINUE.

No, Bryan thought. This wasn't right at all. He hadn't just imagined it this morning. Unless he was also imagining it now. But the slot in the pavement looked real enough, and the words didn't go away no matter how many times he shook his head. Either he had more hormones than any kid in Mount Comfort

Middle School or he was going insane. Or maybe his hormones were driving him insane!

Bryan groaned.

One thing he knew for sure: This day was turning out to be a disaster.

8:07 a.m.
A QUESTION OF SANITY

BRYAN LET THE TIMER COUNT ALL THE WAY DOWN

to three this time before fishing in his pocket for a coin. In part he was waiting for help, for another student to see that he had nearly face-planted off of his bike in the middle of the parking lot. But this was school— either kids were too caught up in themselves to notice or they'd noticed and just didn't care. Nobody came to help him up, so there was nobody to confirm that what he was seeing was really there.

But that wasn't the only reason he let the timer tick down. He was testing it, thinking that if it got down far enough, it would just go away. *Maybe*, he thought, *it if goes down to zero, the slot and the mysterious blue writing will vanish and nothing will happen. Everything will go right back to normal.*

Maybe.

That's what he thought when it hit six.

When it hit four, he got nervous and reached for his pocket anyway, grabbing the first coin he found and dropping it quickly into the slot, then panicking even more. It was a penny. Who ever heard of *anything* costing a penny? Even the old arcade machines his dad told him about always took quarters. But the second Lincoln's face disappeared, so did the words. One coin, it seemed, was as good as another.

Bryan sighed in relief and rolled over, pressing his back to the pavement and looking up at the sky. He made the right choice, surely. Continuing was better than *not* continuing, wasn't it? If you didn't continue, you had to, what, start over from the beginning? The beginning of what? Or maybe you were just finished—whatever *that* meant.

He thought back to this morning, not being able to move his legs. To the words in the mirror. The warnings and messages flashing all around him. He had no idea what any of it meant, why it was happening, but he wasn't ready to test it by letting that timer hit zero. Not yet. Better to feed the slot. At least until he figured out what on earth was going on.

Bryan got unsteadily to his feet and then pulled up his bike to lean against, straightening out its nose. He stood there for a moment, adding it all up in his head. At the other end of the parking lot, kids filed off of buses and moped their way into the building just like normal, sleepwalking to their lockers, meandering, oblivious, to their first class. The popular kids loitered on the steps, congregating like geese, pointing and laughing. Little pockets of kids traded phones and gawked at photos and messages, gulped down caffeinated sodas, frantically crammed for first-period quizzes. It still *seemed* like the same Mount Comfort Middle School, not some alternate, parallel, alien dimension—though most of these kids could be aliens, as far as Bryan knew. He looked at the street, but the cavalcade of ferocious bikers had ridden out of sight. He looked back at the slot in the blacktop. It had disappeared too.

Obviously, he was the only one going crazy. For everyone else it was just another Friday. Bryan watched the hundreds of students filing through the doors, going about their routines. Just following the program.

The program.

Insert coin to continue.

Press any key.

No, he thought. *Absolutely not. Couldn't be. Totally ridiculous.* Bryan pressed his head between his hands as if he were afraid his brains were about to come bursting out his ears, a ludicrous idea taking shape: What if something happened last night, something way beyond weird? What if the two things—the secret level in Sovereign of Darkness and the bizarre start to his day—what if they were related somehow?

Impossible, of course.

More likely he was just nuts.

He needed a second opinion.

He found Oz right where he expected to, waiting by their lockers, looking nervous, like a gazelle listening for a rustle in the plains. "I've been waiting forever. What happened to you?" He pointed to the worn, wet knees of Bryan's jeans and the skinned patches on his arms.

"Slipped on a banana and fell off my bike. But that's not the half of it. We need to talk. I have something important to tell you."

"I know. Me too. I rode on the bus today with Mike McGregor, and he said he overheard Stephen Eldner talking yesterday after school, and—"

"Whatever, my turn," Bryan said, trying to remember who the heck Stephen Eldner was and immediately not caring. "I think my life is a video game."

Bryan stared at Oz. Oz stared at Bryan.

"Huh?"

Bryan took a deep breath and then took Oz by the shoulders. "Okay. Last night I was playing Sovereign of Darkness, and I unlocked the secret bonus level."

Oz's face lit up like a fireworks display. On Christmas. In Times Square. "What? Are you serious? Get out!" He offered a high five. Bryan didn't take it, just kept holding on to Oz, afraid he might fall down otherwise. The whole world seemed off balance. The tiles of the floor seemed to spin.

"No. Listen, Oz. I unlocked it, and then my computer

crashed, and then I woke up and everything was hay-wire, like messed up to the extreme."

"You mean the game."

"I mean my *life*," Bryan said.

Bryan watched Oz's eyes. Saw the glimmer of rec-ognition wash over them. Oz nodded.

"I get it."

"You do?" That was a relief, because Bryan didn't get it at all.

"Of course," Oz whispered. "Role-play. It's Friday, right? A little LARP action to kick off our weekend. We should have dressed up, though. I'll be Secret Agent Yin Kai from the Silent Stalker series. And who are you again?"

Bryan reached up and grabbed Oz by both cheeks, stretching them, pulling his face so close that their noses almost touched. "You don't get it. I'm not play-ing a game. I mean . . . maybe I am, but that's not what I'm saying. This isn't make-believe. I think my *life* is a game." Bryan held his friend in place, ruddy face squished between his hands.

"Ew er whurting my chiks," Oz murmured through fished-out lips.

Bryan let go, looked around, and then pulled Oz even closer to their lockers so nobody passing by could eavesdrop—not that anybody had ever cared what the two of them said to each other before. "Okay. So when I woke up today, I seriously couldn't move my legs, and there was this message, right, in these glowing blue letters hovering above my alarm clock, telling me to insert a coin," Bryan whispered. "So I did."

"Wait . . . insert a what?"

"A coin. You know. Like in those ancient arcade games that old people like our parents used to play?"

"Oh," Oz said, still obviously confused. Bryan kept going.

"So I did, but that wasn't the end of it, because more strange things started happening. Like my clothes are like armor, but not really, and these shoes are, like, average walking shoes. And the orange juice gave me points or something. And then on the way here these bikers tried to run me off the road, and one of them had an evil mustache and threw a banana at me, and I got the coin message *again*. Like I lost or something, and the game was over, but it wasn't, because I stuck in a penny before the numbers could reach zero, and everything was back to normal, except *not* normal because I have no idea when it's going to happen again, or even *if* it's going to happen, only that I've continued twice already, and I'm having a hard time catching my breath, and is any of this making *any* sense to you?"

As he talked, Bryan watched Oz carefully. His best friend's eyes widened in wonder, then narrowed in suspicion, before settling into a look of calm under-standing.

"Yes," Oz said when Bryan had finished. "I think I've got it. You hit your head when you crashed your bike and you have a concussion."

"I didn't hit my head," Bryan insisted. "I mean I did, but that's not what this is about."

"Well, in that case, you've gone right off the deep end."

Bryan shook his head. "I know it *sounds* crazy."

"*Is* crazy."

"But I'm telling you it's true. It's really happening. And I don't know what to do."

"About the mysterious coin slots."

"Yes."

"And the magically appearing electric-blue text messages floating in the sky."

"Yes."

"That apparently only you can see."

"So far."

"And the bikers that want to kill you."

"I don't think they wanted to kill me. Well. Maybe the guy with the mustache wanted to kill me." Bryan ran a hand through his hair. Oz sighed.

"Know what I think? I think you seriously need to cut down on the Mountain Dew," Oz said solemnly.

"You're not helping."

"Maybe you should go see the nurse. Or the school counselor. This is probably stress related. You might need medication."

"Oz . . ."

"My older sister had a similar problem. Started seeing gnomes everywhere. Turns out it was all anxiety. Though I still think she's battier than a baseball game."

"Oz!" Bryan grabbed his best friend by his shirt this time, pulling him so close that he could smell the strawberry Pop-Tart on Oz's breath. "I promise you.

I am *not* making this up. This is happening. To *me*." He locked on to Oz's eyes and held him there, paralyzed.

"Okay," Oz said. Bryan let go.

"So you believe me?"

Oz put his hands up, not quite ready to commit, but probably afraid of what Bryan would grab hold of next; his cheeks were still pink from being tugged on. "All right. Obviously some strange things have happened to you this morning, and they are clearly freaking you out."

"But do you *believe* me?" Bryan prodded. Because if he couldn't count on Oz, then it was painfully clear that he was on his own. And he couldn't handle this— whatever this was—on his own.

Oz took a deep breath, leaned up against the lockers. A small flock of students shuffled by, uncaring. "Okay. Let's say, just for the sake of argument here, that you are *not* a hallucinating, flipped-out nutjob, and that your life *is* now a video game—which is impossible, of course, and, if you don't mind me saying so, a little pathetic, even for us—how do you get it back to normal?"

"I don't know," Bryan said. "I don't even know why

this is happening. Maybe there's something I'm supposed to do. Some, like, I don't know, quest or something I'm supposed to complete."

"A quest?" Oz repeated.

Bryan nodded. "Yeah, maybe. I don't know. Something great I'm supposed to accomplish."

"You mean here? At *school*?" Oz said, clearly not buying it.

"Do you have any better ideas?"

The bell clanged just above their heads, warning them that they had three minutes to get to first period.

"All right," Oz said. "Gym is in, like, three hours. Just try to relax, and see if this whole blue-writing stuff doesn't just go away on its own. If everything hasn't gotten back to normal by lunch, we will figure it out together. Or we will visit the nurse and see if she has any Xanax. My dad takes those when he comes home from work and starts talking to my mom."

Bryan nodded. "Right. Just relax and see if it goes away."

"Are you seeing any words now?" Oz asked.

Bryan shook his head.

"Any coin slots? Counting numbers? Gnomes?"

"I never said anything about gnomes. The gnomes were your idea." Bryan decided if he started seeing gnomes, he would definitely go see the nurse.

"All right. You better hurry. You don't want to be late to Tennenbaum's again." Bryan looked up at the clock. Only a minute left. Math was on the other side of the school, but he could still make it.

"I'll see you in gym!" Oz called after him. Bryan nodded. Gym was only three class periods away. He could make it. After all, it was only school. Familiar, boring, mindless, tedious school.

How bad could it be?

8:23 a.m.
A PUZZLING TURN

"LaTe aGain, Mr. BIGGINS."

The class let out a collective snort as Bryan tried to slip unnoticed through the door, but Mr. Tennenbaum caught him anyway, sporting a serious scowl. Bryan glanced at Tara Timmons, who gave him a sympathetic shrug. Though they never talked outside of school, he and Tara often copied each other's homework, at least on the days Bryan managed to show up on time. Neither of them was a big fan of first-period math.

"Sorry, Mr. Tennenbaum," Bryan said, trying to sound remorseful, though he only sounded out of breath. He had been forced to take a roundabout way to math, having spotted Tank blocking his usual path. Normally, Bryan would have merged with the crowd and tried to slink by, but Wattly had had that look in his eye. Purposeful. Calculating. Or as calculating as someone with six brain cells could be. Given how Bryan's day was going so far, skirting around Tank seemed prudent, even if it did make him extra late to math for the second day in a row. Mr. Tennenbaum was making Bryan reconsider.

"It would be one thing if it only impacted *your* learning, Mr. Biggins. But your tardiness and interruptions affect everyone in the class."

"I understand. I really am sorry," Bryan murmured.

Mr. Tennenbaum eyed him from behind his gold-rimmed glasses, looking down at him past his graying beard. He was wearing the tweed jacket with the button missing and the coffee stain on the sleeve. The math teacher picked up his grade book and clicked the pen that he kept tucked in his shirt pocket, quickly scrawling something down. Bryan couldn't see what it was, of course, but he *could* see the message that appeared from out of nowhere.

-1 HP.

Bryan blinked. There it was, hanging right next to Mr. Tennenbaum's tufted fuzz of hair, almost sitting on his shoulder, except this time instead of iridescent blue, the letters were red, bright as a new stop sign, impossible to miss. They flashed briefly, then vanished.

"What the heck?" Bryan blurted out.

"Excuse me?" Mr. Tennenbaum's face glowed, matching the color of the letters that had disappeared, his eyes now sharp slits. Someone in the class murmured a wincing "ooh," and Bryan quickly backtracked, realizing he had said what he did out loud even though he hadn't meant to. "Sorry. It's just . . . I thought I saw something."

The letters were gone. Nobody in the class made any indication that they had seen them. Maybe Bryan had just imagined them again, but he wasn't imagining the look on Tennenbaum's face. Strained and purple, like a toddler holding his breath.

"You enjoy disrupting my class, Mr. Biggins?"

"No, sir."

"You have a free period this morning, don't you?" Tennenbaum said, biting off each word.

Bryan nodded. "Third period, sir." That was supposed to be Bryan's study hall. He knew where this was going.

"Not anymore," the math teacher said, then proceeded to fill out a detention slip. Someone in the back of the class whispered something about "trouble in the Shire"—the joke that never got old, apparently—and the kids around him laughed. Bryan took his blue slip and found his seat, slumping as far down as he could, still picturing the message that had shone briefly above the math teacher's shoulder.

"Today we will be continuing with our lesson in geometry," Tennenbaum said, stifling his irritation and putting on an air of enthusiasm that he would sustain for all of thirty seconds. Bryan looked at the man, but he couldn't bring himself to listen. He was grappling with those red letters floating in the air.

HP? Horsepower? Harry Potter? A brand of printers? Hit points?

Hit points like *health*? Like in Sovereign of Darkness? Had he really lost a hit point for being *late to class*? If so, how many did he have to start with? And what did that even *mean*, losing one? Was that, like, a day off of his life or something? For being a few stupid minutes late? What happened if he ran out of *all* his HP? How many had he started with? Bryan thought about Kerran Nightstalker. The dark elf had well over a hundred hit points, but Bryan had also leveled him up over days. Weeks. At the start of the game the ranger had had only ten.

This was ludicrous, Bryan told himself. That was Sovereign of Darkness, a charred wasteland infested with demons and monsters, all waiting to bite your head off. This was middle school. There had to be *some* difference.

"Finding the area of three-dimensional spaces, like this room, for example . . . ," Tennenbaum droned.

Calm down. Relax, Bryan reminded himself. It was just one hit point. And he didn't *feel* any different, except maybe his stomach was queasier than before, and his head had started pounding. But he hadn't gotten a "game over," and he hadn't been asked to insert a coin this time, which meant that whatever was happening, it wasn't all or nothing, win or lose. Different games had different rules. He could figure this out.

There was pause in the background noise. Then Mr. Tennenbaum's voice came in sharper.

JOHN DAVID ANDERSON

"Mr. Biggins. Since you must know all of this already, perhaps you can come to the board and enlighten us."

Bryan snapped out of his daze and looked around at the two dozen faces staring at him. Then he looked at the SMART Board at the front of the room. It was full of drawings of three-dimensional objects. Cubes, cones, pyramids, all with arrows and numbers going every which way. Tennenbaum stood next to it, scowling, his stylus in hand.

"Sorry, what?"

"I said, why don't you come up and show us how it's done, since you don't feel like you have to pay attention to what I'm saying."

Another twitter ran through the class, but a hiss from the math teacher squelched it. Tennenbaum motioned for Bryan to come up front. Reluctantly Bryan pulled himself out of his desk and walked to the board, like a prisoner shuffling to the gallows. He took the stylus and stared blankly at the screen.

"Start at the top," Tennenbaum commanded.

Bryan faced the board again, keeping his back to the rest of the class, certain they were all laughing silently at his misfortune. The screen looked like a big jumble. Along the top sat a bunch of formulas that he was vaguely familiar with, stuff they'd been working on like: $V = \frac{1}{3}\pi r^2 h$ and $SA = Ph + 2B$ Though now they looked more like hieroglyphs or alien inscriptions.

"Whenever you're ready," the math teacher said in a smug voice. Bryan held the stylus in his sweaty hand and pressed the tip up against the screen.

He paused. He thought he heard music. Coming from out of nowhere. Voices humming, softly, barely audible, but steadily growing in volume. It sounded exotic, foreign—Russian maybe?—like something men in fur-lined caps might kick-step to. Bryan whirled around to the class, but as soon as he did, the humming stopped. Everyone was just staring at him.

"We're waiting," Mr. Tennenbaum said.

Bryan turned back to the shapes drawn on the SMART Board, and the humming started up again, as if on cue. *Dum. Da-da-dum, da-da-dum, da-da-dum, da-da-dum, da-dum-da-dum-dum-dum.* He was sure he had heard the tune somewhere before. He turned again and it disappeared, but as soon as he faced the board, it began again.

"Any day now, Biggins."

Then Bryan noticed that the shapes weren't normal either. They were no longer frozen on the screen. They were *moving*. They were, in fact, *dropping*. Inching toward the bottom edge of the board. It was a slow and steady march—cones and cubes and spheres incrementally making their way down to the bottom of the screen to the beat of the folksy Russian humming.

Whatever was happening to him, whatever had started this morning with the alarm clock, this was obviously part of it. He needed to solve this problem or risk losing more hit points or getting another continue. Beside him Tennenbaum was tapping his foot impatiently but not in time to the song, meaning either that the math teacher had no sense of rhythm (likely) or that the music was only in Bryan's head (equally likely). Bryan licked his lips and zeroed in on one of the falling shapes. He looked up at the formulas at the top of the screen and then at the cone that was about to drop right off of it. He quickly did the math in his head and used the stylus to scrawl in the answer. As soon as he'd found the volume of the cone, it vanished with a satisfying flash.

Bryan smiled and turned to Mr. Tennenbaum, as if to say, *Got it.*

"Next," the math teacher said.

"Next?"

Tennenbaum glanced sideways at the screen. The other shapes continued their steady decent.

"*All* of them?" Bryan asked desperately.

"We don't have all day," Tennenbaum said with a shrug, looking up at the clock.

Behind Bryan, the humming grew louder. *Da-dum, da-dee-dum, da-dee-dum, da-dum-dum-dum.*

Bryan turned back to the screen, beads of sweat prickling his forehead, the stylus slippery in his hand. He picked a sphere and found its surface area, scrawling the answer on the board. It, too, disappeared, but just as soon as it did, a new one took its place at the top, pushing the rest down. A multitude of shapes filing in columns down the screen.

"You've got to be kidding me," Bryan said under his breath. Then he quickly puzzled through the formula for the volume of a cube, causing it to vanish and another shape—a pyramid—to drop in place above it. The Russian dance music picked up tempo, grew louder, more frenetic. Bryan hunched over, solving one problem after another, the answers coming easier to him now, but the shapes dropping faster and faster. He let one slip by and heard Mr. Tennenbaum click his tongue disapprovingly.

"Missed one."

Bryan tried to ignore it, worked the problems as fast as he could, trying to clear the board, but he couldn't keep up. The shapes didn't change, but the numbers grew more complicated, harder to calculate.

"Time's almost up."

Bryan wiped his forehead on his sleeve with his free hand. The objects were growing fuzzy. He couldn't keep them straight. There was no way he could clear the board of problems. How many hit points would he lose if he couldn't? Would he have to insert another coin? Was this really what this craziness was all about? Geometry? *Really?*

He was about to give up when he noticed a flashing cube at the top of the board. It looked different from the rest. Where the other shapes had simply been outlined in black, this one was multicolored and pulsing. Bryan stopped working on the pyramid that was ready to fall off the bottom of the screen and aimed his stylus at the cube. He needed to calculate its volume.

INSERT COIN TO CONTINUE

Each side was seven centimeters. Bryan struggled to do the math, his brain in overdrive. *Seven times seven times seven. Forty-nine. Three, carry the six.* He could feel Tennenbaum's eyes burrowing into him. The humming had reached a fevered, frantic pace.

"Three hundred forty-three cubic centimeters!" he shouted.

Bryan wrote it in and then pushed down on it with the stylus. Suddenly the rainbow cube vanished, taking all the other shapes with it, as if by magic.

The board was clear.

The soundtrack of Russian folk humming suddenly stopped.

Bryan turned around to look at Mr. Tennenbaum. The math teacher didn't look happy, his whole face pulled downward. But Bryan couldn't help from smiling.

There, hanging in the air above the math teacher's head, was another message written in blue. Two messages, in fact. The first said: **+100 XP**.

And the second said: **LEVEL UP**.

Bryan stood there, at the front of the room, staring at the blue letters as they faded, his whole body shaking. Level up. One hundred experience points. That had to be good, right? It had to mean something. Did it mean he was done? That whatever was happening to him was over? He looked expectantly at Mr. Tennenbaum, as if the math teacher had the answer.

"That will do, Mr. Biggins." Tennenbaum coughed. Then he turned to the rest of the class. "Would anyone else like to try?"

Bryan looked around the room. Half of the students were nearly asleep. The other half were only feigning interest. He wondered if they had even been watching. Wondered why they hadn't cheered him on or at least shown some small sign that they were impressed. Were they really such mindless zombies that they hadn't detected anything weird going on?

Asia Delaney raised her hand to take a turn, and Bryan took his seat, slumping into it, sweaty, heart thumping, watching the board, waiting for her to start. *Let's see how she does*, he thought.

Except Asia Delaney was given only one problem, and it just stayed in the center of the board. It took her almost as long to finish the one as it had taken Bryan to finish all of his. When she sat back down, Bryan leaned over to get her attention.

"You didn't hear anything strange while you were up there, did you? Like . . . I don't know . . . humming Russians?"

Asia Delaney rolled her eyes. "You are so weird," she said.

Bryan nodded and turned back around.

That's what he'd thought.

9:15 a.m.
ROMEO, JULIET, AND THE ZOMBIE APOCALYPSE

WHEN THE BELL RANG, TENNENBAUM TAPPED Bryan on the shoulder on his way out and held him back. The man's morning breath was nearly suffocating. When he spoke this time, it wasn't in his usual voice but a low, husky growl meant for Bryan's ears only.

"When the bell for the third hour tolls," he said, "meet me in these chambers, among the smoke and shadows."

Bryan gave the math teacher a questioning look. "So you're saying I should just come back *here* for third period?"

Tennenbaum nodded. "I shall be waiting."

Bryan nodded back politely—he didn't want to get in any more trouble with the math teacher today—and retreated into the hall. He looked to see Tennenbaum watching him with a disturbing grin. Then the man winked, which was even more disconcerting. Forty-year-old math teachers shouldn't be allowed to wink at their students.

Bryan took a swallow from a drinking fountain and then leaned up against the wall. The day was getting even weirder. Now he was losing HP and gaining XP. He was hearing folk music and imagining falling shapes. He was leveling up, which he took as a positive, except he didn't *feel* particularly level. He felt really unbalanced. Completely out of control.

And to top it off, now he had detention.

He needed Oz's help. But to get that, he had to make it to fourth period.

Bryan merged with the herd and shuffled toward English, keeping his eyes on his Boots of Average Walking Speed, shouldering his Burdensome Bag of Knowledge, made even more burdensome by all the books he'd added, afraid of looking up to see more blue letters sparkling in the air telling him that he had lost this or gained that. He'd made it halfway to C Hall when he finally looked up to see Jess, of all people, standing at the end of the corridor, talking with two of her friends. She had her hair up today, a few strands snaking down either side of her neck. He could see she had earrings on. Dangly silver ones. Her face seemed to glow, as if she had two tiny suns tucked into her cheeks.

Bryan stood back and watched her, half-hidden behind a wall of people, afraid she might see him, or even worse, say "hi" to him. It was hard enough trying to talk to her on a normal day. Finally she ducked into a classroom, and he had to jog to make it to English on time. He sneaked into class just as the bell for second period rang.

Ms. Zinn, the English teacher, sat on top of her desk with her legs crossed like she always did. She was the youngest teacher at Mount Comfort—twentysomething, with bright eyes and long, straight blond hair and a wardrobe full of short skirts, making her maybe the one teacher in the whole school you wished *would* wink at you.

Today, though, Bryan tried not even to make eye contact with her. He tried not to make eye contact with anyone. In fact, he wished he could just spend all of English class with his eyes shut. If you can't see it, it must not be happening. Whatever "it" is. Ms. Zinn waited for everyone to sit before she began.

"Today we're going to continue with Shakespeare's classic tragedy." She paused to accommodate the groans from the class, most from the boys, but some from the girls, too. "To recap from last time, Romeo and Juliet have just met, and it was, of course, love at first sight."

"What a load," came a voice from the back of the room, followed by laughter.

"Just because you've never experienced love at first sight, Mr. Simmons, doesn't mean it doesn't exist," Ms. Zinn chided.

Bryan thought about the stick of lip balm tucked into his dresser, hidden among the rolls of socks. The first day he'd met her—way back in the third grade—she'd sat next to him at their table and said, "I'm Jessica. But everybody calls me Jess." He said his name was Bryan and everybody called him Bryan. She said he was kind of funny. Not exactly *Romeo and Juliet*. But close enough.

Ms. Zinn continued, "Unfortunately, there are numerous obstacles standing in the way of their love, not the least of which is the long-standing feud between their two houses."

"And the fact that nobody can understand what they are saying," someone else added.

"I'm sure everyone in Shakespeare's time understood perfectly well," Ms. Zinn replied. "So open your books to act two, scene two. Perhaps the most famous scene in the entire play. And can I get some volunteers?"

Predictably, nobody raised a hand. Ms. Zinn began scanning the room. Bryan lowered himself into his seat, careful not to look up. *Not me. Not me. Not me. Not me. Not today, of all days. Oh please, gods of not-getting-called-on, if ever there was a time you saw fit in your mercy to—*

"Bryan. How about you be our Romeo today?"

He knew it.

"And . . . Gina. You be our Juliet."

Gina Ramirez looked like a possum trapped

between a pair of high beams, shriveling in her seat. It was clear from her horrified expression that she had no interest in even pretending to fall in love. At least not with Bryan.

"Let's start with you, Juliet. Page forty-two, about five lines from the top."

Gina cleared her throat. Someone in the back whispered, "This should be good," and got an evil eye from Ms. Zinn.

"Whenever you're ready."

Gina took a deep breath, then let it all out in a train wreck of syllables smashed together. "Oromeoromeo. Whereforeartthouromeo. Denythyfatherandrefusethy-nameor—"

"Excuse me, Gina," Ms. Zinn interrupted. "Maybe you could read slower and with a little more passion. Juliet is pining. She is in agony *and* ecstasy. She finally knows what she really wants, and of course it's the one thing she can't have, and she's torturing herself to find a work-around. Let's try it again."

Gina took another breath. Ms. Zinn nodded and smiled encouragingly. Bryan buried his face in his hands but peered through the slats of his fingers. He felt bad for her, but not as bad as he felt for himself. When Gina spoke again, the words were at least comprehensible.

"*O Romeo, Romeo! Wherefore art thou Romeo? / Deny thy father, and refuse thy name; / Or, if thou wilt not, be but sworn my love, / And I'll no longer be a Capulet.*"

There was a pause.

All eyes shifted from Gina to Bryan. "Romeo?" Ms. Zinn prodded.

"Oh. Yeah. Sorry," Bryan said. The class laughed, because anytime a teacher calls you out, it's hilarious. He smiled weakly at Gina and then looked down at his book, an anthology with pages so thin you could see right through them.

Bryan shook his head. Looked again. Thumbed through a couple of pages. He glanced over at the book of the person sitting next to him. Same cover. Same page. But the type in the other person's book was black.

The type in Bryan's book was blue.

And not just any blue. The same color as the messages that appeared from out of nowhere, the ones only he could see. It didn't look like any kind of Shake-speare he had ever seen before.

"Wherefore art thou?" Ms. Zinn prompted, earning another chuckle from the class.

Bryan licked his lips and held his book close to him so no one else could see, though it didn't seem like anyone else cared to. "Ms. Zinn, I'm not sure I can do this."

"It's all right, Bryan. You'll be fine. Just read the words on the page," she said reassuringly.

"Yeah, but I don't think it will be the same as any-one else's," Bryan explained, still staring, wide eyed, at the different-colored font in his book.

"Well, of course it won't," Ms. Zinn cooed. "We infuse the words with our own experience. We make it personal. That's the beauty of great literature: its abil-ity to transcend its own circumstance and speak to us on our own terms. Now come on, Romeo. Come woo your Juliet."

Bryan cast his eyes over to Gina and then back down to his page. He could hear the second hand on the clock over the door ticking away. He read silently to himself first. Right below Juliet's lines was written:

YOU STAND AT THE EDGE OF A GARDEN.
THE CUTE GIRL YOU'RE SMITTEN WITH
STANDS UP ON THE BALCONY, BATHED
IN MOONLIGHT. DO YOU

A. HIDE IN THE SHADOWS AND LISTEN
    TO HER DRONE ON ABOUT YOU
    SOME MORE BECAUSE YOU LIKE
    TO HEAR HOW GREAT YOU ARE?

B. JUMP INTO THE LIGHT AND
    PROCLAIM YOUR UNDYING LOVE
    FOR HER, KNOWING THAT ALL HER
    KINSMEN ARE DETERMINED TO KILL
    YOU?

C. SHOOT HER WITH AN ARROW
    COATED IN A POWERFUL
    SLEEPING DRAUGHT, KIDNAP
    HER, AND DRAG HER BACK TO
    YOUR CASTLE UNDER COVER OF
    DARKNESS?

"C would probably be easiest," Bryan mumbled.

"What?" Ms. Zinn asked. "Speak up. We can't
hear you."

INSERT COIN TO CONTINUE

"Um . . . hang on." On a whim Bryan settled his finger on the first choice. Suddenly, at his touch, new words appeared in his book. These words were in black, however, in the font he was accustomed to, the same font shared by the rest of the books in the class. They were new lines, attributed to Romeo. Bryan's lines.

"Um . . . right . . . okay. *Shall I hear more, or shall I speak at this?*" he said, reading what had just appeared.

Gina Ramirez took her cue from Ms. Zinn and continued, saying something about names and roses and smells. Bryan was only half listening. His eyes grew big again as new blue type appeared on his page.

THE CUTE GIRL ASKS YOU YOUR NAME. DO YOU

A. TELL HER YOU ARE ROMEO?

B. TELL HER TO MIND HER OWN BUSINESS?

C. TELL HER TO CALL YOU LOVE?

Bryan looked at Gina, then at Ms. Zinn, then back at the book. He was pretty sure it wasn't the middle one, and the first seemed entirely too straightforward for Shakespeare, who, Bryan knew, liked to drag things out for no apparent reason. He touched the C, and several more lines appeared. Something about drinking, ears, and the word "love," like, fifty more times. Bryan read them out loud cautiously, scanning ahead, occasionally glancing at Ms. Zinn to see if she noticed anything out of the ordinary, to see if he had chosen correctly, but she wasn't even looking at her book. It lay closed on the desk beside her. In fact, she was staring out the window at the parking lot and the gray clouds gathering above it, caught up in the moment or lost in thought or maybe planning her weekend. Bryan wasn't sure she was even listening. He wasn't sure anyone was listening. Gina stumbled over a line, not daring to take her own eyes from the page.

"I would not for the world they saw thee here," she said.

Bryan looked back at his book.

THE HOTTIE ON THE BALCONY BEGS YOU
TO LEAVE, AFRAID THAT HER KINSMEN
WILL FIND YOU AND KILL YOU. DO YOU

A. TELL HER THAT MAKES SENSE?
   SHE'S JUST A GIRL YOU MET AT A
   PARTY, AFTER ALL, AND HARDLY
   WORTH DYING FOR.

B. MAKE SOME LONG-WINDED, NOBLE
   SPEECH ABOUT DEATH AND LOVE
   AND ALL THAT?

C. TELL HER FAMILY TO SHUT UP
   AND BRING IT, ALREADY? YOU'LL
   FACE THE WHOLE LOT OF THEM.

It had to be B, Bryan knew. That's the way Willy would have wanted it.

And yet.

Bryan looked at Ms. Zinn, still staring out the window. Looked over at the rest of the class, some of them nodding off, others only pretending to follow along as they doodled in the margins of their books. Looked at Gina, whose face was red with concentration or embarrassment or both.

He made his choice.

Romeo's lines appeared. Bryan cleared his throat and read them, uncertainly at first, but then with growing confidence.

"'For thy love, I wouldst now face a thousand blades. / And slay each man who would our path detour. / And so let the name Montague ring out. / And challenge all who would our union bar.'"

Bryan looked over at Gina, who quickly glanced down at her book. Her face creased, as if she'd just seen something strange, a typo or a line out of place. She puzzled over it for a second and then finally she read: "'Some noise stirs within. Dear love, be gone. / Thy shout has awakened all our armored host, / Who bear down on thee, thy blood to spill. / Fly now or all our future days be lost.'"

Bryan saw a strange look pass briefly over Ms. Zinn's face as well. She suddenly turned away from the window and looked from Bryan to Gina, then back again. He was sure she was going to say something. Ask him to stop. Or to read the last part again. Or to show her his book. Or to go to the principal's office. Any of these seemed likely.

Instead she simply said, "Well? Come on? Keep reading!"

Bryan glanced back down. The writing had changed from black to blue again.

> THE GARDEN IS SUDDENLY FILLED
> WITH CAPULETS. THEY SEE YOU AND
> CRY FOUL, CHARGING WITH BLADES
> DRAWN. DO YOU
>
> A.   DECIDE THAT NO CHICK IS
>   WORTH ALL THIS AND FLEE?
>
> B.   PLEAD WITH THE DAME'S
>   FAMILY TO HEAR YOUR SIDE OF
>   THE STORY?
>
> C.   DRAW YOUR SWORD AND FACE
>   DEATH IN TRUE LOVE'S NAME?

Bryan's finger hovered over the first option. After all, they had him surrounded. Let Juliet marry some man named after a French city and be done with it. Then again, this was supposed to be Shakespeare, so death was kind of a foregone conclusion. Might as well go down swinging. Bryan chose answer C, and new lines of black type bubbled up onto the page. He grinned as he read, spitting out the words.

"'Have at thee, then, you curs, you scoundrels. / Taste cold steel and bandy blades o'er words. / Though you may share the name of true love's rose, / You'll e'en share the blood picked from its spiteful thorns!'"

From her place at the desk, Ms. Zinn clapped her hands. Her eyes sparkled. She looked back and forth from Bryan to Gina, waiting breathlessly. Bryan heard the rustle of pages as a few of the other students suddenly grew interested, opening their books, trying to find their place. "Well?" Ms. Zinn asked. Her book still lay closed beside her, but she made no move to open it. Bryan wondered what hers would even say. "What happens next?"

Bryan looked at Gina, who shrugged. He cleared his throat.

"It says, 'Enter Mercutio . . . the ninja.'"

There was a murmur in the class. Bryan waited for Ms. Zinn to say something about there not being any ninjas in *Romeo and Juliet*. Instead she pointed to a boy in the second row. "Michael, you be Mercutio."

INSERT COIN TO CONTINUE

"Sweet," Michael said.

"Well, what are you all waiting for?" Ms. Zinn egged them on. "Keep reading. This is the exciting part."

"Um. Okay," Michael said, scanning down the page, looking a little confused but playing along, doing what he was told. "Uh, let's see here. . . . 'Brother, we are outnumbered ten to one, / Or ten to two, though I do run where others walk / And Capulets do crawl, and with one flick / Of finger scratch a dozen cats and send / Them chasing o'er tails. Have at you!'"

Someone in the back of the class gasped. Michael made some motion with his hand, as if he were actually wielding an imaginary sword, brandishing it about in the face of a wave of snarling Capulets. Bryan took his cue and thrust with his own imaginary sword, then stopped to read: "'One, two, three more slain. / My blade is tipsy having drunk the blood / Of so many cowardly Capulets. / See now, how e'en darkness has its due. / And blots the moon as Tybalt comes to dance.'"

"Tybalt! Tybalt! Who's Tybalt?" Ms. Zinn fluttered

impatiently, leaping up off her desk now and pacing back and forth.

"I will be," a boy named Rodrigo said, raising his hand.

"Then read! Come on. Let's have it!"

Rodrigo read his line with a menacing growl. "'Wretched boy, grave injuries you have caused / With sharpened tongue and steel. But words nor swords / Can shield you from my dragon's sharpened claws.'"

Bryan checked his book and his eyebrows shot up.

TYBALT, JULIET'S COUSIN, ENTERS
RIDING ON A GIANT BLACK DRAGON
SPOUTING FIRE. DO YOU

A.   RUN FOR YOUR LIFE?

B.   USE YOUR KNOWLEDGE OF
     ARCANE MAGIC TO SUMMON THE
     FAIRY OBERON TO DEFEND YOU?

C.   LET THE DRAGON EAT MERCUTIO,
     THEN SLAY IT AND ITS RIDER
     WHILE IT'S DISTRACTED?

"You're riding a dragon?" Bryan said, looking over at Rodrigo, who just shrugged, as if to say, *Guess so.* Granted, Bryan had never read *Romeo and Juliet* before or seen any movie versions, but he was pretty sure there weren't any ninjas or dragons in it. But if any of his classmates noticed, they didn't care. Maybe this was all part of whatever it was that was happening to Bryan. Or maybe they were just glad that Shakespeare's play had finally gotten interesting. That certainly seemed to be the case with Ms. Zinn.

"Ooh, a dragon," she whispered, eyes like saucers. "Exciting!"

Bryan looked over his options for dealing with the dragon, then glanced at Michael. "Sorry, man," he said.

"Sorry for what?" Michael said. Then he looked down at his own book. "Oh."

Michael threw his hands into the air and pronounced, "'Alas, am I to be a dragon's meal, / A morsel, tidbit, trifle to the last? / The teeth. The claws. 'Tis more than just a scratch. / A plague on both your houses! I am slain.'"

"'And I am slain!'" Rodrigo/Tybalt said, clutching at his heart.

"'We are all slain!'" said the rest of the class in unison, picking up seamlessly on their cue, mimicking the voices of a dozen Capulets, supposedly skewered at the tip of Romeo's sword.

"'And we are still in love,'" Bryan and Gina said together. Then Bryan glanced down at his text to see the stage directions.

ROMEO and JULIET kiss.

He looked up at Gina. Forced a smile.

"We can probably skip that part," he said.

She nodded, maybe a little too emphatically. Bryan looked back at his script.

The slain bodies of MERCUTIO, TYBALT, and other CAPULETS begin to stir.

What the heck does that mean? Bryan thought. Then Gina broke in with the next line.

"'O Romeo, we must depart,'" she cried, suddenly caught up in the moment, or maybe just relieved at the not kissing. "'The sickness boils in our kinsmen's blood. / And soon, though soul be split from flesh and heart, / Still flesh will rise anew, but viler still, / To walk the night. And so we must make haste. / For I can sense the rotten carcass rise.'"

Suddenly Mercutio's voice piped in. "'To eat the brains of those we now despise,'" he said, doing his very best zombie imitation, hands stretched out and everything.

Exeunt.

There was silence.

Bryan just sat there.

Apparently, act 2, scene 2 of *Romeo and Juliet* ended with the two lovers fleeing for their lives from a pack of reanimated corpses. Gina had a horrified look on her face. Most of the other kids in class looked confused, though a few of the boys seemed genuinely impressed. Bryan closed his book quietly.

Ms. Zinn smoothed out her short plaid skirt with both hands.

"That was . . . ," she began, giving pause for Bryan to fill in all the possibilities—ludicrous, insane, just *wrong*.

"Exhilarating," she finished. "Thank you, every-one, for your impassioned reading. Especially you, Mr. Biggins. Well done." Then she turned to the board and began to scrawl something in chalk.

Above her head Bryan watched the letters appear, just as they had last period with Mr. Tennenbaum.

+50 XP.

For winning Juliet's heart while killing her entire family and slaying her cousin's dragon. For being willing to sacrifice Romeo's best friend, Mercutio—the ninja—just so he could get the girl. For slogging through Shakespeare in second-period English. Fifty experience points.

Ms. Zinn turned around, still beaming. "Now for the rest of the class, I'd like you to get out your notebooks and write about why you think Shake-speare chose the zombie apocalypse as an appro-priate backdrop for his tragic love story, and how the walking dead act as a metaphor for our own inhumanity."

Bryan heard her words, but he wasn't really lis-tening.

He was staring at the blue letters, already starting

to fade, thinking that reading Shakespeare had taught him two things this morning.

First: People did crazy, stupid stuff for love.

And second: Whatever it was he was supposed to do to make this all go away, he needed to do it quick before things *really* got out of control.

10:27 a.m.
LOUNGE RAIDER

BY THE TIME SECOND PERIOD ENDED, BRYAN HAD written exactly one sentence in his reader response journal. It had nothing to do with true love or zombies or inhumanity. It simply said, "What is happening to me?"

He didn't have an answer.

In an hour he could talk it over with Oz. That was what they'd said. Wait to see if things resolved themselves, and if not, they would work through them together. Or seek professional help. Things certainly hadn't resolved themselves. If anything, they had gotten more compli-cated. Gym was only one period away. But first Bryan had to get through detention.

He opened Mr. Tennenbaum's door as the strag-glers in the hall behind him shuffled past, hoping that maybe the math teacher would be acting normal.

"Shut the door, my son."

So much for that.

Bryan stood in the doorway and stared at the man, sitting at his desk, huddled over a stack of papers. The blinds had been closed, and all but one row of fluorescent lights had been turned off, draping Mr. Tennenbaum in a pool of sickly yellow and casting his shadow along the wall. He had his back turned, but even from the doorway Bryan could tell what the math teacher was doing. The fog around him was thick. The smell overpowering.

"Are you *smoking*? In *school*?"

Tennenbaum spun in his desk chair and squinted at Bryan. A pipe hung from the corner of his mouth, bil-lowing up tendrils of white smoke. The math teacher stroked his unwieldy salt-and-pepper—predominantly salt—beard.

"Please, Master Biggins," he spoke through clenched teeth. "I asked you to close the door."

Master Biggins? That was a first.

Bryan rolled his eyes but did what he was told. He was already firmly planted on Tennenbaum's bad side. "I'm pretty sure you can't do that here," he said, pointing at the pipe.

Mr. Tennenbaum took the pipe from his mouth, regarded it for a moment as if it were some strange artifact he'd just unearthed, then stuck it back in its corner with a considerable huff. "And *I* am fairly certain that I shall do whatever I wish." The math teacher manufactured an impressive white ring and watched it dissolve in the air between them. "I trust you are here to atone?"

Atone? That didn't sound good. Apparently, Tennenbaum was going to make a big deal out of this. "Yeah. Listen, I'm sorry about being late to class, and I promise I won't do it again, but I'm having this really strange morning, and I thought, if it was all right with you—"

"Silence!" Tennenbaum roared, causing Bryan to take a step back, pressing up against the door. The math teacher held the bowl of his pipe, pointing the gnawed black tip at Bryan. "This is no time to blabber about, boy. There is important work to be done. A task has been set before you."

A task. Terrific. Bryan was going to spend the next hour cleaning erasers or sorting papers. Or something worse. Tennenbaum motioned for Bryan to come closer. The smell of smoke wove its way through the room, pungent and acrid, stinging Bryan's eyes. The math teacher opened the top drawer of his desk and fished out a black cloth pouch, barely large enough to get his hand into. He dug with two fingers and plucked out a handful of quarters. Bryan shuddered. The last thing he wanted to see right now was more coins.

"Six pieces of silver," Tennenbaum said. "You will need them to unlock the treasure."

Bryan looked at the coins. Were these quarters he was supposed to use to continue? Did Tennenbaum know what was going on? And what did he mean by "treasure"? He tried to sum up all these questions with a "Say what now?"

"You must journey to the room that is forbidden

to those of your kind," Tennenbaum continued, his voice scratchy with phlegm. "The sanctuary beyond the hall. Where the elders gather in repose."

Bryan shook his head. Sanctuary? Elders? Forbidden to his kind? "You mean the *teachers' lounge*?"

Tennenbaum nodded sagely, setting the quarters on the desk between them. "There you must retrieve the cake of gold from its prison of glass."

"Cake of gold," Bryan repeated, even more bewildered.

The math teacher put up a crooked finger. "But beware. The path will be fraught with danger. The Eye of Krug is watching."

Eye of Krug . . . Eye of Krug . . . Bryan wracked his brain. Did he mean *Amy* Krug? One of the hall monitors? She was known to patrol during third period. And she wore thick glasses. "You could just give me a hall pass, you know . . . ," Bryan began.

The math teacher fixed him in a stern gaze. "You must go unarmed!" he insisted. "I can grant you no protections, offer you no wards. You will not need your pack." Tennenbaum pointed to Bryan's backpack. "And know that the vault itself is not unguarded. Within it sit three creatures of the most hideous disposition. Reynolds, Wang, and Baylor-Tore." Tennenbaum practically hissed the names.

Bryan repeated them in his head. "Mrs. Reynolds the music teacher?"

"They are not to be trusted," Tennenbaum warned. "Do not fall victim to their web of lies."

Bryan laughed. This had gone from bewildering to ridiculous. Whatever Mr. Tennenbaum had put in that pipe, it had obviously shot straight to his brain and done some rearranging of what it found there. Bryan put his hands on the math teacher's desk. "Listen, Mr. Tennenbaum, I know I screwed up, and I can't keep coming in late to class. And I'm more than happy to sit here and do extra math problems or help you grade quizzes or whatever, but don't you think this is a little, you know . . ."

"Dangerous?" Tennenbaum finished, a hint of mischief in his eyes.

"I was going to say 'silly.'" Actually, he was going to say "stupid," but thought that might be pushing it.

The math teacher's eyes widened. "The cake of gold must not be broken. Only once it is returned, pure of form and devoid of imperfections, will you be free to continue on your path." Then he stuffed the pipe back between his lips and nodded again, leaning back and half closing his eyes behind his gold-rimmed spectacles. "I have spoken," he said through clenched teeth.

"Yeah, but wouldn't it be easier if you just took the money and went down to the teachers' lounge yourself—"

"I HAVE SPOKEN!" Mr. Tennenbaum roared, lunging forward and slamming a fist on his desk, nearly causing his half-empty coffee cup to topple off the corner.

"Right," Bryan whispered, adding "*pushy old fart*" so low that Tennenbaum couldn't hear. Then he scooped up the quarters, stuffed them in his pocket, and slowly backed away as another ring of smoke drifted lazily between them.

"Remember the Eye of Krug. Beware the guardians three. Return with the cake of gold," Tennenbaum chanted as Bryan walked backward through the room.

"Eye of Krug. Guardians three. Cake of gold. Total *nut*case," Bryan whispered. He escaped through the door and took a much-needed breath of fresh air, the smell of tobacco lingering in his nose, the clink of six quarters jangling in his pocket.

INSERT COIN TO CONTINUE

Obviously, Tennenbaum was even crazier than Bryan was. Still, it could have been worse. Breaking into the teachers' lounge was at least better than scraping gum from the underbellies of student desks. Besides, Bryan now had something to hold over the crotchety old math teacher's head. Smoking in school was cause for suspension for students, so it couldn't be too good for teachers. But first he would go get this stupid treasure. After all, he could only assume there was something in it for him as well. Maybe this was the quest he was meant to complete. Maybe this was how he would finally get his day back to normal.

The teachers' lounge was on the first floor close to the art room. He was on the second. He would have to take the stairs and then circle around. Bryan walked down the hall, passing a few kids who had been kicked out of their classrooms for one reason or another, heads bent over whatever menial task served as their punishment. One of them looked up at Bryan from the book he was reading.

"Beware the Eye of Krug!" the kid whispered, then huddled back over his dog-eared copy of *A Wizard of Earthsea*.

Bryan looked at him oddly. "What?"

"I didn't say anything, dweeb," the boy said, burying his nose farther into his book.

Of course he didn't.

Bryan shook his head and slowly made his way to the stairs. As he descended, he ran over the names Tennenbaum had listed. The ones he was supposed to watch out for. *Reynolds. Wang. Baylor-Tore.* He knew Mrs. Reynolds. Ms. Wang he thought might be the eighth-grade science teacher. He didn't know any Baylor-Tore. Maybe she was new this year. He exited the stairwell, lost in thought, eyes watching the progression of marble tiles on the floor, still struggling to make sense of it all. Finally he chanced a look ahead.

There she was, standing at the end of the hall with her hands on her hips. As if she had known he was coming. As if she had been waiting for him.

Amy Krug.

She stood there in her black Mary Janes with her pouty, purplish lips. Hall monitor and perennial library volunteer. President of DARE and two-time treasurer of the student council. Beloved by teachers everywhere and mocked by half the student body for the way she sucked up to anyone in authority, like a Dyson on a power surge. She was dressed in a business suit—the only girl at Mount Comfort Middle School who owned one, let alone wore it to school—black to match her raven hair, which was pulled into a taut whip, snapping like a hooded cobra behind her. She glared at Bryan with dagger eyes behind her thick, black-framed glasses. He stopped in his tracks.

Bryan wasn't in the half that mocked Amy Krug. He actually kind of admired her tenacity. He knew that someday she'd score a full scholarship to an Ivy League university and win a Nobel Prize, coming back to Mount Comfort to rub it in everyone's faces. Maybe, underneath it all, she was even nice. But seeing her there, at the end of the hallway, staring down at him along her hawk's beak of a nose, mouth curved upward in a smug little smile, he panicked.

Beware the Eye of Krug.

"I see you, Biggins," she said in her grating voice.

She took a step toward him.

"I see *everything.*"

Bryan turned and bolted back up the stairs, pulling himself along the handrails. He paused halfway up, listening to the sound of Krug's shoes clicking down the hallway. *Clip. Clop. Clip. Clop.* The Eye was on the move. Walking steadily. Like a hockey-masked killer in a slasher film.

Bryan made the turn and paused at the entrance to the upper hall, stopping to catch his breath. "This is stupid," he whispered to himself. "What's the worst she can do?" On a normal day she would just write him up or send him to the principal's office.

But today was no normal day, and Amy looked like she was ready to tear somebody's head off. Bryan pushed through the door to the second floor and listened for the slap of Krug's soles on the stairs. No sound save for the droning voices of teachers lecturing behind closed doors. He waited a second more just to be sure. Probably she was there at the bottom, waiting for him to descend, the patient spider sitting at the edge of her web. He would have to take the long way again.

Bryan looped around the cafeteria to the east wing, taking the opposite stairwell and exiting near the gym, stopping to peek around every corner just in case. He could hear the thud of balls bouncing off the walls.

He'd be back here in less than an hour—provided he could get Tennenbaum's little treasure without getting caught. As he walked, he kept his head down and his eyes up, hoping nobody would stop him and ask him what he was up to. It helped being a mostly good kid. His permanent record was clean. The two teachers he passed didn't give him a second look.

He turned down B Hall and stopped, ears prickling at the familiar sound.

Clip. Clop. Clip. Clop.

Bryan felt a chill run through him from scalp to heel. He looked around frantically. The sound reverberated down the hall, increasing in volume.

Clip. Clop. Clip.

There she was. At the other end. Head swiveling, Terminator style, as if she were scanning for life forms. As she twisted his way, Bryan ducked through the first door he found, throwing his back against a wall and shutting his eyes.

He was safe. For the moment. He heard water running and opened his eyes.

Tile floor. Paper towel dispensers. Sinks. Stalls. Lots of stalls.

JOHN DAVID ANDERSON

Only stalls.

He wasn't safe. He was in serious danger.

"Are you really *that* stupid?" a voice said.

A tall, skinny Asian girl, clearly an upperclassman, stood by the row of sinks drying her hands and looking over at Bryan with disgust. Bryan backed himself into a corner, putting his hands up. Forget the "sanctuary beyond the hall." He was trespassing on truly sacred ground now.

"Uh. Oh. Sorry. I was just, um, looking for the teachers' lounge."

The girl gave him a hard look. "Right. Because the girls' bathroom is where *all* the teachers hang out. They keep the coffeemaker in the last stall." She rolled her eyes, finished drying her hands, and shouldered Bryan out of the way, shaking her head. "Creep."

"Sorry," Bryan whispered again, making sure that he was out of visual range while the door swung open. When she was gone, Bryan sighed and shook his head, then crouched down to inspect the stalls. No feet. The place was empty, at least. He couldn't help but notice how much cleaner the girls' bathroom was. There were no puddles on the floor from errant aim, for one, and the sinks weren't clogged with paper towels. Only the graffiti was the same: hierarchical lists of both girls and boys by their relative cuteness and popularity. He noticed Jess's name was on three of the lists. Ms. Zinn was even on some. Landon Prince graced the top of several. Bryan's name was nowhere to be found.

He stood by the entrance and pressed his ear to the door. He could still hear her moving out there. *Clip. Clop. Clip.* Getting closer and closer still. The hairs on Bryan's arms stood up. The footsteps stopped right outside the girls' bathroom.

She's coming in. She knows I'm in here. Maybe the other girl had told her. Or maybe Krug just sensed it. He looked over at the stalls, wondering which one to hide in, afraid that she would hear him if he tried to move, afraid that somehow, at least today, the Eye of Krug could see through cinder block. He held his breath for ten seconds. Twenty.

And then . . . the clop of black Mary Janes retreating back down the hall. Fading.

Bryan's heart hammered as he peeked outside. The hall was clear. Krug was nowhere to be seen and the teachers' lounge was just down the hall with the door half open. He couldn't stay in the girls' bathroom any longer; it was totally creeping him out, not to mention he was afraid of someone else catching him here. Bryan counted to three and burst through the bathroom door, scrambled down the hall, and practically dived into the teachers' lounge, then turned and shut the door softly behind him.

He listened for a moment, then sighed. No sign of Krug. He turned to take in the room.

The sanctuary. It wasn't much to look at, actually. Refrigerator. Microwave. Sink. Vending machine. Stained carpet. Peeling paint. On the far wall was a poster with a hot-air balloon and a message telling whoever cared to REACH HIGHER. Someone, presumably a teacher, had Sharpied in a doodle of a man dangling from the basket by one hand, ready to plummet to his death, and the message FALL FARTHER. The whole place smelled of coffee and Mexican food.

In the center of the room sat a scratched-up laminate table surrounded by three middle-aged women, each huddled over an early lunch. Bryan recognized Mrs. Reynolds instantly—her characteristic beehive hairdo and heavily lipsticked pout were unmistakable.

And he had been right about Ms. Wang—she was the science teacher—a scarecrow of a woman with sunken cheeks and frizzy black hair that might have been styled via electric socket. The third figure he had seen only once and guessed to be Baylor-Tore. Judging by her size, he guessed she was the new boys' wrestling coach. Or school security. She slightly resembled a gorilla, with moderately less hair.

None of the three of them bothered to look up. Instead they all stared blankly at one another across the table, spooning or shoveling their meager meals into their frowning mouths. Reynolds was sucking down low-fat Greek yogurt. Wang was sawing through a Weight Watchers chicken breast congealed in what could be mushrooms. Baylor-Tore was just looking at celery stalks. She had a row of them, all lined up. The teachers stared ominously ahead, each at the other, like Capulets risen from the dead—mindless yogurt-, celery-, and rubber-chicken-eating zombies. Bryan didn't even garner a glance.

"Um, hey," he said, feeling the urge to break the silence, to get them at least to acknowledge that he was in the room. After all, he was a student. It would be

JOHN DAVID ANDERSON

like an antelope nosing around a lion's den. They should have shooed him out instantly, but they didn't seem to care. Like most everyone else today: completely zoned out. "I just need to get something for Mr. Tennenbaum and then I'll be out of here," he explained. The teachers didn't respond. Baylor-Tore blinked once. Wang poked at her chicken slab wordlessly.

"Okay, then," Bryan said, then maneuvered around the table to the vending machine in the corner. He scanned all the selections, just to be sure, but there really was nothing else that could be mistaken for a cake of gold. The package containing a single Twinkie sat in the center row. D-3. It was a dollar. Mr. Tennenbaum had obviously overestimated the going price for golden treasure.

Bryan looked at the coin slot and shuddered at the memory of the last two he'd encountered—even knowing coin slots *belonged* in vending machines didn't make him feel better. He reached into his pocket for the quarters Tennenbaum had given him and dropped four in, listening to the rhythm of their descent, turning each time to see if the expressions on the women's faces had changed, if they cared he was there.

Mrs. Reynolds slurped her peach yogurt with a sickening, slow, slick sound. *Sssccchllrrrrrrp.*

Bryan tried not to watch. He punched in D-3. "Come on, hurry up," he whispered. The wire uncoiled. The cake of gold inched forward.

Schllrrrrrrp.

And then it got stuck. Snagged on a corner of its cellophane package.

"No. No. No. No. No. Not today."

He would have said something worse, but there were teachers present, even if they didn't seem to be listening. He punched the buttons again and again, then grabbed both sides of the machine, looking to shake it, except it was way too heavy. The Twinkie didn't budge. He took a step back, then rammed his shoulder into the vending machine glass.

-1 HP.

Bryan rubbed his sore arm and glared at the already-fading red letters hovering in the air before him. The cake of gold remained suspended behind the glass force field.

"Forget this." He fished in his pocket for what was left of his change. Not counting the quarter he'd fed

JOHN DAVID ANDERSON

to his alarm clock, he had started the day with two quarters, a dime, and three pennies to his name, one of which had gone into the parking lot after the bike crash. Adding Tennenbaum's other two coins to his own, though, he had enough. He dropped another dollar's worth into the machine and typed in the code. The coil turned, and not one but two packages dropped into the bin below. Double cakes of gold. Bonus buy. Sort of. Bryan bent down and thrust both hands through the flapping door, pulling his treasures free. Finally.

He was about to apologize to the teachers for having interrupted their lunch when he heard a hissing from behind.

"Cakessssss . . ."

Bryan twisted around slowly. The table in the center of the room was empty now. The yogurt abandoned. The chicken half eaten. The celery still in formation. The three teachers were all up out of their chairs. They were looking at Bryan.

The languid zombie trance they had been in had vanished. Their eyes were now sharp slits, their coffee-stained teeth bared. Mrs. Reynolds had her head cocked to one side, watching him, curious, catlike. Ms. Wang was nearly crouching, her spine arched, hands on the back of her chair. Baylor-Tore was blocking the door. She could easily block two of them. Bryan clutched the two packs of Twinkies to his chest.

"Hello, ladies," he said.

"The *caaakesss*. We must have the *cakesssss*...," they all said in hoarse whispers, two of them circling around the table, creeping toward Bryan, their hands stretched out before them. Ms. Wang's nails looked obnoxiously long and were painted the color of rust or dried blood. Mrs. Reynolds's head kept twitching uncontrollably as she sniffed the air. "You must give them to us."

Bryan pointed to the vending machine. "Um. There's still another package in there."

"We will share them, *yessss*?" Mrs. Reynolds hissed.

"Yes. Share them with you, we will. Delicious *cakesss*," Wang agreed.

Tennenbaum's words echoed in Bryan's head. *Beware the guardians three. They are not to be trusted.*

"Yeah, I'm sorry. They aren't really mine to share. I really... I really should just go." Bryan made a move

JOHN DAVID ANDERSON

to get around, but Mrs. Reynolds mirrored him, cutting off his escape.

"They are not yoursssss," she hissed.

"Trespasser!" Ms. Wang croaked. "Bandit. Thief. You are not welcome here."

"Gives us the cake-sees," Baylor-Tore added in her unusually deep voice from her spot by the door, licking her lips voraciously. "We wants them!" The other two teachers were on either side of Bryan now, closing in with wide, wild looks in their eyes. You weren't allowed to touch students anymore, he knew. You couldn't even hug them without a parent's permission. Still, he couldn't shake the feeling that these three were about to tear him to pieces. They continued to advance, slowly, pressing him farther into the corner. Reynolds licked the tips of her teeth. Wang opened and closed her clawed hands. He had to do something.

Almost instinctively, Bryan lunged forward, dodging the swipe of Wang's ragged nails, holding both packages of Twinkies with one hand and reaching out for the table with the other. He grabbed the first thing he could, wrapping his free fist around it. He could sense Mrs. Reynolds right behind him, nearly on top of him, but he spun around, holding his weapon out toward her.

"Stand back!" he cried.

"Hisssssssss!" Mrs. Reynolds brought her hands up in front of her face and instinctively cringed from the stalk of celery Bryan was waving back and forth. Both teachers bared their teeth and squinted, but they slowly backed away.

Bryan took a step forward, pointing the celery from one to the other, forcing them into the corner by the vending machine. He thrust and they clawed, trying to swipe the deadly vegetable out of his hand. Bryan quickly turned and glanced at the door to try and figure some way to get past Baylor-Tore and out of this nest of monsters.

Except Baylor-Tore was no longer guarding the door.

Just then two beefy brown arms closed around him, one of them wrenching the celery stalk from his hand, sending it flying into the wall. Baylor-Tore bear-hugged Bryan and lifted him off of his feet, swinging him back and forth like a pendulum, roaring in his ear. *"Givesss us the cakesss!"*

The celery gone, the other two teachers swooped in. Bryan kicked out with his feet, trying to keep them

JOHN DAVID ANDERSON

at bay, feeling their hands on his legs, reaching for him, clutching at him. His right arm was pinned to his chest, but his left hand—the one holding both Twinkies—was still free.

He realized then what he had to do. He had no choice.

He brought one package to his teeth and frantically tore through the top, releasing the sickeningly sweet scent of cream-filled sponge cake, then flung the open pack as far as he could, careful to keep hold of the other. The open Twinkie hit the wall and slid down, leaving a splotch of its white innards on the painted cinder blocks.

Bryan felt his feet hit the floor as Baylor-Tore released him, then he watched as all three teachers bolted for the dessert, scrambling over one another, clawing at one another's faces, growling like wild animals. He watched in horror as Mrs. Reynolds sank her teeth into Ms. Wang's leg to keep her from reaching the Twinkie.

Bryan ran. Only Wang turned and scowled as he scrambled to his feet and headed toward the door. He pushed his way out, giving no thought to Amy Krug or anyone else, just wanting to get as far away from the teachers' lounge as possible. He glanced down both halls, then he ran all the way back up to Mr. Tennenbaum's room, ignoring the shouts of the other teachers he passed, commanding him to slow down. He burst into the room and flipped on the overhead lights, causing the math teacher to stare at him through shielded eyes.

"Blast it, boy, don't you have the sense to knock?" Tennenbaum asked, setting his pipe down and leaning back in his chair.

Bryan slammed the door closed and stepped up to the desk, tossing the remaining package with its lone Twinkie on top of it. "You should have told me they were *dieting*," he said through ragged breaths.

Tennenbaum smiled mischievously. "I'm surprised you made it out alive," he said. Then the math teacher looked down at his desk and frowned.

Bryan followed his gaze. The clear package was nearly pressed flat, the cream leaking out the sides, completely pancaked. It must have happened during the escape, perhaps when Baylor-Tore tried to crush him to death.

"I warned you. The cake of gold was not to be broken. Pure and devoid of imperfections."

"Dude . . . you weren't there. It was everything I could do just to get away. They tried to *bite* me." Bryan started to explain, but the math teacher cut him off. He picked up the smashed package of sponge cake and tossed it in the wastebasket.

"I am afraid . . . you have failed," he croaked.

"But I got your stupid cake," Bryan protested.

"Be gone."

"You can still lick the inside of the package."

"I said BE GONE!"

The math teacher looked at Bryan with burning red eyes.

Bryan had so many other things he wanted to say, but he bit his tongue. He picked his backpack up from where he'd left it and headed for the door, eager to be out of the room, away from Tennenbaum and the cloud of smoke that hovered around him, but the handle wouldn't budge. The door was locked.

Then Bryan noticed the slot set into the door. The words flashed above, right next to the narrow paneled window.

INSERT COIN TO CONTINUE.

Bryan dropped his head. "Seriously?" Reluctantly

he dug in his pocket as the timer started counting down. He had only three coins left. At the rate he was going, he'd never make it through the day. He dropped a dime in the slot and the timer stopped with eight seconds to spare.

He turned back to Mr. Tennenbaum, who had swiveled around and was staring out the window, where the blanket of dark clouds had finally unzipped, loosing fat raindrops that thumped against the panes. Bryan couldn't help it. He had to ask.

"Do you know what's going on here? What's happening?" he said to the back of the math teacher's head. "Because if you do, please tell me. I don't understand what I'm supposed to be doing, or why everything's different, or why everyone's acting so weird. It's all just a big, jumbled, confusing mess, and none of it makes any sense at all."

Bryan watched as a tendril of smoke wove itself into a halo over the math teacher's head. It was a full ten seconds before the man spoke.

"Welcome to middle school, my son," Tennenbaum said. Then he pointed behind him with the tip of his pipe. "Be sure to shut the door behind you."

11:20 a.m.
CALL OF DODGEBALL

BRYAN LEFT MR. TENNENBAUM WREATHED IN A crown of smoke, then quickly made his way back toward the gymnasium, all the while listening for the sound of Amy Krug's shoes clunking across the floor. He met Oz by the boys' locker room. His best friend looked like an overinflated balloon, barely able to contain himself.

"So you won't believe what Chris Smith told me in Spanish today. I mean he *said* it in English, but we were *in* Spanish—," Oz sputtered the moment he saw Bryan.

"I was just attacked by a pack of teachers who wanted my Twinkie," Bryan interrupted.

"Wait. When did you have a Twinkie?"

Figures that *that* would be the sticking point with Oz. Bryan ignored the question. "Oh, and Mr. Tennenbaum thinks he's Gandalf. And Mercutio's a zombie. And I've gained a hundred and fifty experience points and leveled up once, though I don't have any idea what that means. And needless to say, I'm still seeing things. And sometimes hearing them. And you're right—I am *completely* crazy." Bryan looked at Oz, waiting for a response.

"Do you still *have* the Twinkie?"

"No, I don't still have the Twinkie! Did you hear what I just said?"

"Okay. Just asking. So I guess you're still having a bad day."

"Yeah. You could say that."

"Then I probably shouldn't tell you that Chris heard Micah talking to Olivia Walker, who said that Landon Prince was going to ask Jess to be his girlfriend tonight."

Bryan felt a pain in his gut, instant and crushing. "Did she say yes?"

"Did who say yes?"

"Jess. I mean, did Chris say if Micah said whether Olivia knew if she was *going* to say yes?"

"Dude, it's just a rumor. And it's not like you don't have more important things to worry about. What was the part about zombies again?"

"Long story. Written by Shakespeare. You had to be there."

Bryan moped his way into the boys' locker room, Oz in tow, both of them finding a space as far from the other boys as possible. Locker rooms were death traps: You certainly didn't want to get caught with your pants down. As they changed into their gym clothes (thank God there were no mirrors in the changing area as he replaced his Tunic of Unwashing with what was probably a Tank Top of Infinite Stinkitude), Bryan relayed as much of his morning as he could, starting with his challenge at the SMART Board and ending with his harrowing escape from the teachers' lounge. He left out the part about ducking into the girls' bathroom. He knew Oz would have way too many questions about it.

"I can't believe Ms. Wang attacked you," Oz marveled. "She seems so nice."

"I'm just telling you what happened. Between them

and Tennenbaum and Amy Krug, I feel like half of the school is out to ge—youch! What was that for?"

Bryan rubbed the red spot on his arm where Oz had just pinched him. The red letters appeared above Oz's head.

-1 HP.

"Thought maybe you were dreaming."

"I'm not dreaming, all right? First off, if I were dreaming, you would be part of that dream and wouldn't be able to pinch me to see if I was dreaming."

"Unless I'm just a part of the dream and you're dreaming that I pinched yo—ouch!"

Oz rubbed his arm this time.

"This isn't a dream," Bryan insisted. "Something majorly freaky is going on, and I need your help figuring it out."

"I *am* trying to help."

"Pinching is not helping."

"Tell me about it," Oz said, inspecting his arm.

From outside the locker room they heard an unfamiliar adult voice yell for everyone to hurry up and get out there.

"We better go," Oz said.

Bryan tied his shoes, then had a thought, reaching into the back pocket of his Breeches of Enduring Stiffness and pulling out one of his pennies, tucking it into the cuff of his sock. Oz gave him an inquisitive look. "Just in case," he said. Then he and Oz filed out with the rest of the seventh graders. Bryan spoke over Oz's shoulder. "So what do you *think* she will say?"

"Who?"

"Who? Jess who."

"About what?"

"About Landon Prince!" Bryan snapped. Sometimes talking to Oz was like trying to suck Jell-O through a straw. And not a normal straw. The kind people use to stir coffee with.

"Oh." Oz shrugged. "I don't know. What would you say if you were a teenage girl and Landon Prince asked *you* out?"

Bryan didn't bother to answer.

"Come on now, hurry along," boomed the unfamiliar voice. The gym looked different today. Several wrestling mats had been propped up, creating temporary walls. Two carts full of basketballs sat to one side. A man in too-tight gym shorts and his own tank top, revealing copious amounts of armpit hair (hormones had obviously been good to him), came up behind them.

"Hello, everyone. My name is Mr. Kilton, and I'm your substitute gym teacher today. Mr. Gladspell says that since it's Friday and it's raining, we get to spend the whole period playing deathball."

"Did he say 'dodgeball'?" Oz whispered.

"He definitely did not say 'dodgeball,'" Bryan whispered back.

"I've already had two of your classmates volunteer to be team captains," Mr. Kilton explained. "So they will choose teams. Go ahead, boys."

The substitute gym teacher nodded to Reese Hawthorne and Max Trilling, easily the two tallest kids in the class and both on the junior varsity basketball team. Bryan sighed. He was pretty sure the process of choosing teams had been outlawed in every other school across America, but not at Mount Comfort. He was never picked last, at least; that honor always went to Charlie Miner, who had a serious weight problem and a tendency to wipe his snot on his sleeve. Still, you always knew where you stood in the social pyramid when it came time to pick teams in gym. Max looked at Reese and told him he could go first.

It was no surprise that Reese Hawthorne picked Kyle Paul, a solid brick of a kid who was shaped like a pro wrestler. Probably Hunter Warrick would go next. He was a baseball player and part of the inner circle of cool jocks that Reese and Max belonged to. Max and Reese would take turns gathering their friends, and then they would reluctantly sweep up the dregs. Like Bryan and Oz.

"Oswaldo," Max Trilling said.

Oz's jaw dropped. He pointed to himself in disbelief, but Max nodded, smiling. "Yeah, you. Get over here, man."

Oz looked at Bryan, eyes wide with wonder. Oz was almost never picked before Bryan, and neither of them had ever cracked the top ten before. "Huh," he said, then walked a little cautiously over to stand beside Max.

"Hunter," Reese called out as the logical second pick went to join the other team. Bryan saw Oz reach up and whisper something in Max's ear.

"Biggins."

Bryan pointed to himself just to be sure, though

there were no other Bigginses in the school or even in the whole town. Max nodded in affirmation, and Mr. Kilton urged Bryan to move already. He gave Oz a strange look as he walked toward him. Something wasn't right. The two captains continued to call out names, building their squads.

"Gavin."

"Juan."

"Mike."

"Charlie."

Charlie Miner stumbled over to stand beside Bryan. He was already sweating, but he was also smiling. He wasn't last, probably for the first time in his life. In fact, there were quite a few popular kids still left to go. Bryan tried to return the smile, but he couldn't. Something terrible was happening. And by the time every kid had been chosen, it was obvious to everyone, even Charlie Miner.

"They stacked the deck," Bryan murmured to Oz, looking out over the other team. Nearly every kid on Reese Hawthorne's team was at least three inches taller than the kids on the opposite side, a battalion of student athletes with necks as thick as telephone posts. The only serious weapon Bryan's team had was their own team captain.

Max Trilling looked across the gym at Reese and smiled.

"It's a trap," Oz whispered.

Mr. Kilton stepped to the center, in between the two groups, and raised his hands.

"You know the rules. Get hit and you're out. Catch the ball and the other guy is out. We've added a few obstacles to keep things interesting, but they won't last, and once they're down, they stay down. Also," he added, pointing to the carts of basketballs, "I couldn't find the rubber play balls you guys usually use, so we are going to have to make do with these today."

"*Basket*balls?" Juan Delgado gulped. On the opposite side of the center line, Bryan saw the members of Reese's squad nod in sadistic appreciation. "Won't those hurt when they hit us?"

"So don't get hit." Mr. Kilton stepped back beside the carts. "Let the battle begin!" he roared, then simultaneously blew his whistle and tipped the carts over, spilling two dozen basketballs onto the court, rolling toward both sides. Bryan saw one of the balls spin in his direction and contemplated going for it—maybe get a shot in before anyone on the other team was armed—but just as he was about to take off, he felt a tug on his arm.

"Take cover!" Oz yelled, pulling Bryan across the gym toward one of the propped-up wrestling mats.

Bryan looked to see most of his team doing the same, retreating toward the back of their half of the gym, ducking behind the foam and vinyl barricades that were barely standing of their own free will.

All except for Max, who stood right up on the midline—the battle line—calmly bending down and snatching a basketball, palming it easily. Most of the other balls had been snagged by the opposing side, but they hadn't thrown any yet. Max Trilling, the team captain, leader of the dregs, stood defiantly in front of the other captain, Reese Hawthorne. They exchanged nods. Max casually lobbed his basketball across the line. Reese caught it easily.

Mr. Kilton blew his whistle and pointed.

"Guess I'm out," Max said with a shrug. He turned around to face Bryan and the others, who had their heads peeking out from the mats like timid mice. "It's all up to you guys." He grinned. Bryan heard a tremor of laughter from the other side of the gym as the full weight of what had happened—and what was about to happen—descended.

"You set us up, you jerk!" Oz shouted.

Beside them, Rajesh Tambe, a kid that Bryan had once gone to summer wilderness camp with, stood up, seething with anger, thrusting his arms in the air. "Traitor!" he screamed, shaking a fist at Max. "You cheating—"

Boom. Raj went down. Dropped like a sack of flour, the sniper's shot bouncing off his face, leaving its red imprint like a bloody sunburst on his cheek. Head shot. Insta-kill.

"Man down! Man down!" little Stevie Richter screamed from the barricade opposite Bryan, rushing to Rajesh's side, but in doing so he accidently knocked over the wrestling mat, exposing him and three other kids as targets. The sky was suddenly filled with orange.

Stevie took a ball to the chest and another to the leg, stumbling once before smacking the floor, the sound of sweaty skin slapping against laminate. A kid named Marcus Stover, who was one of the Capulet zombies from Bryan's English class, dived to avoid one shot, which barely missed his heel. Mr. Kilton blew his whistle and pointed to signify that he was out. When he turned to protest, he took a second shot to the head and crumpled like a used Kleenex. Bryan looked to see DeShawn Murray bump fists with Reese. Bryan ducked back down behind his mat.

"Marcus is gone," he said.

"We are pinned down," Oz replied. "We need reinforcements."

"There are no reinforcements, you fool!" Juan Delgado screamed. "We're cut off!"

More balls flew. Bounced off the mats. Off the back wall. Off the heads and bodies of Bryan's teammates. Rajesh had managed to crawl to the sideline, where he propped himself against the bleachers, head in his hands. Some of Bryan's other teammates managed to avoid the hail of basketballs fired across the gym, diving and rolling or simply landing with a wet-sounding thud. A few of them picked up balls of their own, tossing them with all their might—but it was a fruitless endeavor. The platoon of jocks on the opposing side easily sidestepped them or caught them, not only scoring kills but reloading in the process. Reese's team didn't even bother to crouch behind their mats. They didn't need to. They crowded the line like a firing squad. It was a massacre.

Mr. Kilton blew his whistle again and again. Pointing to some kid writhing on the ground and then to the bleachers, ordering him off the field of battle. A basketball careened off one poor boy's chest right into another's, taking them both out.

"Double kill!" Hunter Warrick shouted from across the line.

All around him Bryan heard the hollow *thunk* of balls, the steady percussion of widespread annihilation, as he and Oz huddled together, watching the bodies pile up. Basketballs whizzed by, thrown with deadly velocity. They bounced off the gym mat, pummeling it, threatening to knock it over before rolling back to the enemy's side. Bryan looked over at the bleachers. His half was already full of the wounded, many of them doubled over in pain. The other side had only two players sitting down, and one of them was Max Trilling, traitorous team captain, who had given up the charade and gone to sit with his friends. The gymnastics mat buckled under a steady salvo of balls. More of them rained down from the ceiling as Reese and his squad tried lobbing them over the wall like grenades. One of them nearly got Archie Goldman in the leg.

"They've got air support," Oz said as the lobbed balls inched closer.

Bryan chanced a look over the edge of his barricade, then ducked back down as two basketballs nearly took his head off. He looked at the others. There were only five of them left. Giant orange orbs rained down from the ceiling. "We can't hold out much longer," he said. "We're going to have to fight back."

"Againtht them?" Archie protested, speaking with a lisp through the roller coaster of wires that served as his braces—newly acquired two days ago. "We will get thlaughtered."

"I'd rather go out fighting, wouldn't you?"

"No, not really," Oz said. "I'd rather just hide here and wait for the game to end." Sitting beside Oz, barely keeping his body behind the barricade, Charlie nodded his assent.

Juan shook his head. "Bryan's right," he said. "We have to engage."

JOHN DAVID ANDERSON

The five boys looked at one another. Finally Archie nodded. Charlie made a cross over his chest. The basketballs continued to pound, rebounding off their makeshift fortification.

"All right," Bryan said, trying to sound braver than he was. "On my mark we storm the barricade and bring the pain. One . . . two . . ." He started to stand up.

"Wait," Oz commanded, pressing a hand to Bryan's mouth. "Listen."

Bryan stopped. He listened. The only sound was the *bu-bu-bu-bum* of one lonely basketball dribbling, rolling, coming to rest in a corner. The gym was otherwise silent.

"They've stopped," Oz said giddily. "It's over. The battle is over!"

Oz stood up, his white T-shirt a symbol of surrender, the armpit stains a symbol of their struggle. But something didn't feel right. Bryan reached for him by the back of his shorts, trying to pull him down without pulling them off. "Oz . . . no . . . wait . . ."

It was too late.

Bryan watched the sky darken. They came from everywhere, one right after the other, blotting out the harsh fluorescent glow of the track lights above, like a fusillade of cannonballs shot from a galley's broadside, striking Oz in the arms and chest. Oz twisted, stepping backward, throwing his hands up, rocking and reeling with each blow. To the shoulder, the knee, the stomach, the poor boy whipped around like a rag doll in a Doberman's jaws.

"Nooooooooooo!" Bryan screamed as the last ball struck, smashing Oz in the nose. A spray of blood splattered his cheek and shirt. Oz spun once, looking at Bryan with wide, sad eyes. Blinked once.

"Ouch," he said.

Then he collapsed.

Bryan stood up and kicked over the wrestling mat, staring coldly across at Reese and his men, all of them grinning maliciously. The other team was temporarily unarmed—all the balls were on Bryan's side of the line now—but they didn't seem to care. Beside him Bryan heard Archie scream, a guttural, primal sound, even through the braces. Bryan saw the Popsicle stick of a boy scoop one ball and throw it two-handed, soccer-goalie style. His aim was terrible, the throw was low, but the kid on the other team made the mistake of trying to catch it and missed, taking it on the shin instead. Juan also managed to score a hit with his first throw, striking Hunter while his back was turned, laughing about something. Mr. Kilton blew his whistle and pointed, sending them both to the sideline.

Some of Reese's men started to fall back.

Bryan grabbed a ball and flung it as hard as he could. Ricardo Torres leaped to avoid it, but not in time. It just got him on the leg. He was out.

The blue writing appeared above Ricardo's head momentarily as he slouched to the bleachers.

+10 XP.

Bryan's first kill. The taste of it, the sound of rubber striking flesh, the stench of everyone's sweat, the blue words—it ignited something in him. He scrambled for another ball and heaved it, not even aiming, just throwing. It went mostly sideways toward the bleachers, nearly taking Max Trilling's head off; he had to duck to avoid it. But Bryan didn't see it. He wasn't watching where the balls he threw actually went. He was just throwing them. One after another. Load and reload. Fire at will. Blind rage overcame him. He somehow managed to score two more kills, including a head shot of his own as Zachary Owens stooped over to grab a loose ball and took a blow to the ear.

Bryan lost all sense of his surroundings. He didn't see Archie go down, hit in the leg. Or notice when one of Juan's balls was caught, sending him to the sideline. Or when the last barricade, the one Charlie had given up and hidden back behind, collapsed, exposing him to a flurry of balls that simply couldn't miss. Bryan didn't notice any of this. He just scrambled for one ball after another, until there were no more balls left on his side.

And that's when he realized he was alone.

The remnants of Reese's team—there were still five of them—each held a basketball to their chest. They lined up in the middle, Reese at their center.

"A noble effort, Biggins," Reese said. "But you had to know you were going to lose."

Bryan glanced over at the sideline, where his warriors leaned against one another in crumpled heaps, heads on shoulders, noses smeared in snot and blood. Someone had thought to drag Oz over and hand him a tissue. They all looked at Bryan, and a few of them nodded gravely.

Do it for us, they seemed to say.

JOHN DAVID ANDERSON

He would. He would do it for them.

Bryan turned back around just in time to see the lone ball—Reese's ball—hurtling toward him.

He shut his eyes and threw out his hands. Felt something hard and unforgiving burn past them, slamming him in the chest, causing his heart to stop.

Then he heard the whistle blow. Bryan opened his eyes to see Mr. Kilton pointing at Reese Hawthorne and then at the bench. "You're out!" the substitute gym teacher said.

"*What?*" Reese cried.

Bryan held the basketball in front of him, stunned. The squad on his side of the bleachers erupted in a cheer as Reese kicked a stray ball, sending it soaring. Another flash of blue appeared above the boy's head.

+10 XP.

Bryan held the ball up in triumph and turned to his teammates, his brothers. Those he would honor with his victory. Reese was out. Bryan had actually caught the ball for once. "Yeah! Yeah! That's what I'm talking about!" It was glorious.

Juan Delgado pointed, a look of terror on his face.

Bryan turned.

Four more balls, one after another, headed his way at optimum velocity. The first one somehow hit him in the armpit as he twisted. Then the leg. Then the chest. Bryan's vision was filled with orange, followed by red.

-2 HP.

-2 HP.

-3 HP.

The last one got him in the head, rebounding hard above his ear, filling his skull with a dull roar.

-5 HP.

Bryan dropped to his knees, then slumped over to his side. He heard the roar of Reese's men. Heard someone tell him to "Take *that*, hobbit." Heard the double whistle blow, marking the game's end.

Somewhere amidst all the ringing he heard Jess's voice asking him if he was busy tonight. Saw an outline of her standing over him, but it wasn't her now, it was her four years ago, in the third grade, handing him his valentine, the one with the candy heart. He tried to pull himself up, but it was as if his legs refused to move, just like this morning. Everything was blurry. His cheek burned. The floor was slick with sweat. He blinked once, twice, then looked beside him at the inch-long slot that had been carved into the laminate board, about three feet from his nose. The words just hovering there.

INSERT COIN TO CONTINUE.

The timer already counting down. Already at ten. He reached down for his sock, blindly, unthinking, digging for the penny that he had tucked there. The timer was down to five. Bryan pulled the coin free and dragged himself on his elbows to the hole in the floor, inch by painful inch, grunting at the effort.

He dropped it in with two seconds to spare.

He waited for everything to go black. He wanted to pass out. To wake up in the nurse's office, or better yet in his bed at home. But he didn't. He had made it in time.

The game was over, but Bryan was still playing.

12:11 P.M.
ANGRY CHICKENS

OZ'S NOSE HAD STOPPED BLEEDING BY THE TIME
the fourth-period bell rang. Bryan's bruised and bat-
tered team had spent the last ten minutes of gym in
a slumping heap, while Reese and his men had shot
baskets and called one another names. At one point
Mr. Kilton strolled casually over to the bench, asking
Oz if he needed to go see the nurse. Oz shook his
head.

"That's the spirit. A little blood loss never hurt anyone," the substitute gym teacher said.

Bryan was pretty sure that wasn't true—in his

experience blood loss was usually accompanied by pain, sometimes lots of it—but he didn't say anything. He couldn't shake the thought that maybe it had all been his fault. That if he hadn't come to school today, none of this would have happened. They wouldn't have had a sub, maybe. Or they wouldn't have played *death*ball. Raj wouldn't have one cheek the color of a strawberry. Charlie wouldn't be whimpering in the corner. Whatever he was going through—whatever *this* was—he had dragged all of them into it. He wondered if Oz was thinking the same thing. His best friend looked at him from behind his bloody tissue.

"Nice catch, at least," he said in a nasally voice, fingers clamped tight between his eyes.

"Thanks."

Bryan looked at the smeared blood on Oz's cheek. At the floor rash on Juan's chin. At the bump already bubbling up from Charlie's head. The one catch hadn't prevented him from having to drop another coin. He was only halfway through the school day and he'd already had to continue four times. He wondered how many he had left. Maybe as many as he could afford.

Maybe he could continue forever. If that was the case, he was going to need more money.

At the sound of the bell, Bryan helped Oz get to his feet and hobble toward the locker room to change into a shirt that was stained with grape jelly instead of blood.

"Good job, everybody," Mr. Kilton sang to them, clapping his hands. He looked at Bryan specifically. "You can't win 'em all, kid."

Bryan frowned. He wondered which of them he *could* win.

"Come on," Oz said, pulling him along. "I'm starving."

Lunch at Mount Comfort Middle School was the same as at any school: noisy and nauseating, with a 30 percent chance of thrown food. The tang of meat loaf hung in the air whether it was meat loaf day or not, and you had to dodge the ketchup packet land mines that littered the floor. But even for all that, Bryan didn't mind it. It was one of the few times during the day when you could talk to your friends about stuff that mattered, like what you were going to do over the weekend and who'd gotten kicked off the reality shows you watched and how it would be fun to have a Wookiee as a pet, especially if it really could pull people's arms out of their sockets.

Or maybe you could talk about how your life had turned into a giant video game.

Bryan hesitated as he turned the corner on their way to the cafeteria. The incident in the teachers' lounge, followed by crushing defeat in gym, had put him even more on edge, looking for an ambush from every angle. He half expected the cafeteria to be transformed somehow, maybe laid out in a grid with little balls of food set in crisscrossing rows along the floor, and students running around, frantically gobbling them up while the lunch ladies chased them around wearing bedsheets and making ghost sounds. Or maybe there would be a series of platforms he would have to jump across just to get his chocolate milk.

But the cafeteria looked normal. People sat at tables and played with their food and talked way too loudly, just like always. The same clusters and cliques. The same satellite kids wandering around looking for an empty seat. Maybe lunch would just be lunch. He got in line behind Oz.

"Chicken nuggets or lasagna with crumbled pork topping?" The lunch lady's apron was smeared with some sickly-looking brown stain.

"Nuggets?" Bryan ventured.

"Peas or creamed spinach?" School policy required students to pull items from every food group whether they ate them or not. Every day Mount Comfort Middle School wasted enough food to feed half of Uganda.

"I'll just take a banana," Bryan said, playing his "Substitute a fruit for one thoroughly unappetizing vegetable" card.

"Potato chips or corn chips."

"Corn chips."

"You don't want the corn chips," the lunch lady said, waving him off. "They've been sitting under the heat lamp too long. They're like rubber."

Bryan had chewed enough rubber last period when he took a basketball to the face. He switched to potato.

Tray in hand, Bryan found the table where Oz was waiting for him. He had made the critical error of getting the corn chips and was already starting to stack them into a little tower on his tray. He wasn't alone. Myra was sitting at the table too, fiddling with a chicken nugget and watching Oz build with a devious smile on her face. She looked up at Bryan and her smile faded to a pout, a sympathetic one. Her hair was purple today, Bryan noticed. It changed every three days or so, depending on her mood. Purple. Dandelion yellow. Fluorescent green. Never anything that didn't glow in the dark. On magenta days you didn't want to mess with her, but purple was safe.

Myra was pretty much the only girl that he and Oz hung out with—mostly, Bryan knew, because she humored them, but also because there was no one else she could stand to sit with at lunch. Plus there was the little crush she had on Oz, for reasons Bryan couldn't immediately grasp. Minus the chameleon hairdo and the triple-pierced ears and her inexplicable love for bands with names like Deathgasp, Zombie Fetus, and Napalm Bloodbath, Myra was fairly relatable for a girl. She had read every graphic novel ever written and was an absolute beast at Call of Duty. Not to mention she had striking green eyes that glimmered beneath the layers of black mascara. Bryan sat down and Myra stared at him as if she were waiting for something.

"She knows," Oz explained. "I got her up to speed."

Bryan looked back and forth from Oz to Myra, wondering if he should bother being mad. But the truth was he trusted Myra. They would have had to tell her anyway or kick her out of their lunch table. Besides, Myra was smart. Smarter than either Oz or Bryan. Maybe smarter than them combined. He could use her help. He pushed his plate aside and spoke in a whisper. "He told you everything?"

"He told me enough. He told me about the Twinkie."

Of course he did. "Forget about the Twinkie," Bryan told her. "The Twinkie is the least of my worries. He told you about the flashing words? And the game? Sovereign of Darkness? And the coins?"

Myra nodded.

"She agrees with my diagnosis," Oz added.

"Your diagnosis?"

"Yes. We've concluded that you are a paranoid schizophrenic suffering from delusions of reference precipitated by an acute persecution complex," Myra said.

Bryan shook his head. "Cute Percy what now?"

"She means it's all in your head," Oz summarized, pointing helpfully at his skull, just in case Bryan didn't know where his head was located.

"Except it's *not* all in my head," Bryan complained. "You were there at gym. You saw what happened. And the crazy bikers. And Shakespeare's zombies. Mr. Tennenbaum—"

"Mr. Tennenbaum's always been weird," Myra said dismissively. Oz nodded in agreement. He took a chunk of pork topping and set it on top of his corn chip tower. Bryan looked at his tray. He had zero appetite. He offered his bag of potato chips to the first taker. Oz snatched them eagerly. Myra shook her head and continued, "So nobody else has said anything to you, noticed anything strange?"

Bryan shook his head. It was like they were all a part of it somehow. Or they were just that out of it.

"C'mon, man. It's middle school. What do you expect? Half the kids around here aren't even *awake*." It was true. At the next table over, a kid named Terrance Whitley had fallen asleep with his head on his tray and had a corn chip stuck to his cheek.

"Still, we can't ignore the possibility that you are

having hallucinations brought on by some kind of psychotic episode," Myra speculated. "Maybe beating that stupid video game and then having your computer fritz out on you created a breakdown in your mental processes, prompting a kind of dissociative fugue."

"Do you think maybe you could use words with fewer syllables?" Bryan asked. "My head already hurts."

"Sorry. I like to read about mental disorders online. It makes me feel normal, relatively speaking. Basically what I'm saying is you've gone bonkers," Myra concluded.

Bryan shook his head. "I'm not crazy. And I'm *not* imagining things." At least, he didn't think he was. He couldn't be imagining *everything*. Yes, maybe he was making it out to be worse than it was, but there was no question that he had woken up this morning and the rules had changed. Whatever was happening to him, it was really happening.

At least, he thought it was.

Wasn't it?

Myra reached over and patted his hand. "We believe you," she said. Then she elbowed Oz in the side.

"Of course we do," he said, half choking on a potato chip.

They could just be humoring him. In fact, Bryan was pretty sure of it. But at this point he would take whatever support he could get. "So what's the alternative? To my being nuts?"

Oz and Myra looked at each other, then back at Bryan. "Well," Myra began, making her nugget do little cartwheels across her tray, "the alternative is that you really *are* somehow stuck in a video game version of your own life, I guess." She didn't sound at all convinced.

"Which is pretty cool, if you think about it," Oz added with a greasy smile.

"You said earlier it was pathetic," Bryan reminded him.

"That's when I thought you were just making it up. But if you *aren't* making it up, I think it's cool."

"Either way, crazy or not, I think the solution is the same," Myra said. Bryan looked at the two of them expectantly.

"Beat the game," she said.

"Beat the game," Oz echoed.

"Beat the game," Bryan whispered to himself.

"Break the illusion, the hallucination—whatever it is. Pull yourself out of it by getting to the end and accomplishing your goal. Like Sybil reuniting her split personalities."

"Or Darth Vader turning against the emperor and saving his son."

Myra snorted and turned to Oz, still wielding her chunk of chicken. "It's nothing like that," she said.

"It's *kind of* like that," Oz countered.

"Really, it's not. You can't bring everything back to *Star Wars*."

"I disagree, Your Worshipfulness," Oz said.

"Who's Sybil?" Bryan asked, interrupting them.

"She was the famously crazy wom—never mind," Myra said. "The point is you're having some difficulty dealing with reality, which is completely understandable."

"Yeah. Reality bites," Oz concluded, trying to actually bite into one of his corn chips. His teeth couldn't break through. Myra ignored him.

"So you have to overcome whatever it is in your head or your life or whatever that's causing all these problems. Confront whatever little demon is inside to get everything back to normal."

"Confront the demon. Beat the game," Bryan repeated.

"And bring balance to the Force," Oz added.

Bryan looked over at Myra, who just shook her head. "Okay. Assuming I'm *not* just making this all up, how do I do it?"

"Well. Think about every video game you've ever played. What has the goal always been?" Myra asked.

"To get the high score?" Bryan said.

Oz snarfed some of his milk. It dribbled down his chin. Myra laughed. Any other girl would have made a disgusted face. "Seriously?" Oz said. "This isn't Space Invaders. Besides, you haven't said anything about a score yet."

It was true. If there was a score of some kind being kept, Bryan didn't know what his was. He had no idea *how* he was doing, except he was gaining experience points and losing hit points. And he felt perpetually sick to his stomach. And he had only a dime left to his name. "I leveled up once," he offered.

Myra nodded thoughtfully. "Good. That's progress," she said. "So it's a role-playing game, then."

"Except you're you, which makes it *the* lamest roleplaying game ever," Oz said with a snort. He noticed the look on Bryan's face. "Sorry. I'll shut up now." He added another layer to his corn chip tower.

"So like any role-playing game, you go on quests, right?" Myra said, earning a nod from Bryan. "Well. Let's see, you've already uncovered some treasure."

"A cake of gold," Bryan added.

"A Twinkie," Oz clarified, forgetting that he'd promised to shut up.

"And you battled some monsters in the gym," Myra said.

"They were jocks."

"Potato, potahto," Oz said.

"And we lost," Bryan added.

"Let's not focus on the details," Myra told him. "But you're right. You lost. So maybe there's something more important you're supposed to do. Something major. Like, life-changing. Something you've been wanting to do for a while now."

"Like slaying the dragon," Oz suggested.

"Last I checked there were no dragons in Mount Comfort," Bryan said. Of course, last time he checked there weren't dragons in *Romeo and Juliet*, either. He needed to keep an open mind.

"How about your crazy neighbor who smokes too much?"

"Mrs. Fernsworth?" Bryan thought about it. That old bat *did* have rough, scaly skin, and the little kids did call her the Dragon Lady with her shrewd yellow eyes. But no. "I don't think I'm supposed to kill my neighbor."

"Then maybe you are supposed to take over the school. Lead a rebellion—students against teachers. Topple the evil empire." Oz's eyes grew wide with the possibility.

Myra shook her head. "You're such a doofus," she said, flinging one of her chicken nuggets at Oz's tower of pork-topped chips, missing it by inches. He stuck out his tongue at her. "This isn't about us, Oz. This is about Bryan. It's his life. There's something *he's* got to face. Some deep-seated issue he's got to grapple with." She turned back to Bryan. "You weren't locked in the basement as a child, were you?"

Bryan shook his head.

"Who knows," Oz said, "maybe you are supposed to save the world or something."

Myra snorted this time. "Let's not get carried away.

This is Bryan we are talking about." She turned and frowned. "Sorry."

"It's all right," Bryan said.

Oz gave Myra another dirty look as a second chicken nugget nearly missed his sculpture. Then he shrugged. "Maybe it's not that big of a deal at all. Maybe you just have to get through the day."

Just get through the day. Bryan looked up at the clock hanging over the cafeteria entrance. There were still three more hours. Plenty of time for plenty of terrible things to happen. He had already used four continues. He'd forgotten how many hit points he'd lost. Still, getting through the day seemed like a reachable goal. Much easier than saving the world.

There was a sudden groan from Oz as his corn chip tower collapsed, the last of Myra's chicken nuggets having soared through the air in a perfect parabola and smashed into its middle, causing the whole thing to spill over the table and onto the floor.

"Woohoo," she said. "Chicken one. Chips zero."

"You sank my battle-chip," Oz joked. The two of them locked eyes for a moment, Myra probably sending subtle messages, Oz probably missing them entirely. Bryan ignored them both. He was chewing over everything they had just said. About repairing the schism. About beating the game. Facing the demon. Dealing with reality.

And getting through the day.

"This can't be happening," he said out loud.

"It will be all right," Myra assured him. "You just have to learn the rules of the game. And then you have to play better than anyone else."

"Is that, like, a quote or something?" Oz ventured. "Tiger Woods or Tom Brady?"

"It was Einstein, genius," Myra said, punching Oz on the shoulder. Then she motioned toward the clock. Lunch was almost over and Bryan hadn't eaten a thing. They all stood and walked to the conveyor. "Whatever's going on, we will help you. Right, Oz?"

"Absolutely," Oz said. They put their trays up on the belt and turned to leave.

And ran right into Tank.

"Oh yeah," Oz mumbled from behind Bryan. "There is something I've been meaning to tell you."

Chris Wattly was dressed in his football jersey and boots like normal. It looked like he was wearing pads, too, though Bryan figured that might just be how big the kid's shoulders actually were, like you could land helicopters on them. Bryan looked down at Tank's size-twelve feet. He imagined his head being crushed beneath them.

"We need to talk, hobbit."

Bryan took a step back, afraid Wattly might somehow spear his heart on that beefy finger he was jabbing him with.

"Listen, Tank, today is not the best day, all right? I'm going through this . . . thing . . . and I really can't deal with you right now." Bryan winced as soon as he said it. It didn't come off nearly as sniveling and apologetic as it needed to.

"Maybe you should have thought about that before you said what you said," Wattly shot back. Bryan swallowed hard, then chanced a look up. Tank's face was bright red. Bryan had obviously done something to tick him off. For real this time. Something besides just existing, though he couldn't begin to think of what.

"Why don't you back off?" Myra said, stepping up beside Bryan, standing as straight as her purple bristles of hair.

"Why don't you butt out, you raccoon-eyed freak?"

"Hey, don't talk to her that . . . ," Oz started to say, taking a ginger step forward, but a glare from Wattly froze him in place. Tank turned back to Bryan.

"I would just take care of it right now. Except I can't risk another suspension. So instead *you*"—finger in Bryan's chest again—"are going to meet *me* by the Dumpsters behind the diamond today after school. Four o'clock."

Bryan's insides twisted. "Tank, really, whatever this is—" he started to say.

"You show up and we settle this. But if you don't, I will make the rest of your year a total nightmare. Understand?" Wattly smiled, then patted Bryan on the cheek. As he walked away, he held up four fingers as a reminder, not only of the time, but probably also of how many of Bryan's limbs he intended to break. When he was out of earshot, Oz called him a few choice names. Myra rolled her eyes.

"What was that all about?" she asked. Bryan turned toward Oz. He had that look he sometimes got: puppy with a torn tennis shoe in its mouth.

"Oz?"

Oz stared up at the ceiling. "Yeah. So. Remember yesterday in gym when you said that Wattly was a fat, stupid, knuckle-dragging troll who smelled like old farts and would someday end up changing the oil in your car?"

Bryan groaned. "I remember saying that to *you*." It had been a small part of their gym-time conversation, in between Oz's request that Bryan reconsider going to Missy's party and his *begging* Bryan to go to Missy's party. "What did you do, Oz?"

"Nothing. I swear. I mean, I might have told Sheffly. But he promised not to say anything."

"*Dave* Sheffly? *Loudmouth* Sheffly?"

"We were talking about some of the kids on the football team, and he told me how once he got wedgied so hard that his underwear elastic ripped, and I told him about what happened between you and Tank by the lockers and what you said at gym, and then, I don't know, somehow it got all the way to Kirsten Flowers and then to most of the eighth-grade volleyball team, and by then the message had, you know . . . gotten a little mixed up."

Bryan groaned. "Mixed up? How, mixed up? What does he think I said, Oz?"

Oz shuffled his feet. "Maybe something about him being an oily, farting gorilla who eats farts and whose mother . . ." Oz's voice trailed off. "Never mind, you don't want to know."

"No. Please. What did I say about his mother?" Bryan had said plenty of things about Chris behind his back, but he'd never said anything about Mrs. Wattly. He wasn't that stupid.

"You might have said that she was so dumb she couldn't put M&M'S in alphabetical order." Oz winced.

Myra snorted. Then she tried to make her face serious again. "Sorry."

"*What?*" Bryan shouted, then noticed just how many other kids in the cafeteria were watching and lowered his voice. "I didn't say anything like that!"

"I'm sorry, Bryan. I tried to warn you this morning, but then you came in telling me how you almost died falling off your bike and something about a coin and the game and . . . I guess I just forgot."

"I am so dead," Bryan said, leaning up against the conveyer packed with lunch trays full of untouched lasagna and unnaturally pliable corn chips.

"You're not dead," Myra tried to reassure him.

"You're maybe a little dead," Oz amended.

"Listen," Myra said, putting her hands on Bryan's shoulders. "It's only twelve thirty-five. We still have a few hours before we have to worry about Wattly. Let's just get through the rest of this day, and we will deal with this other situation when we get to it. What do you have next period?"

"Social studies," Oz said. It was one of the classes he and Bryan shared.

"Right. Okay. What could possibly go wrong in social studies?" Myra said, then instantly frowned.

Behind him Bryan heard a scream. He turned to see one of the eighth-grade boys slouching toward a table full of girls, arms stretched out, head half twisted, tongue lolling, obviously pretending to be a zombie, like something straight out of *Romeo and Juliet*. The boy licked his lips and moaned, dragging one leg behind him. The girls shrieked and giggled, then they began throwing food at him, pelting him with a barrage of peas until he pretended to fall down.

"So immature," Oz said just as the bell for fifth period rang.

12:37 P.M.
THE END OF THE WORLD

WHEN THEY PARTED IN THE HALL, MYRA GAVE
Bryan a hug, then went to hug Oz, but their trajectories crossed and he ended up nearly punching her in the face. "I'll see you both in band," Myra offered, the only class all three had together. The last period of the day.

Right before I'm destroyed, Bryan thought. *Provided I even make it* that *long.*

"I'm sorry," Oz said as they walked to fifth period. He smiled at Bryan, fishing for a smile in return, but he wasn't going to get it. Bryan knew he couldn't stay mad at Oz forever, but he figured a few years was easily justified.

"I just don't see why you have to go around telling everybody everything." Not that anything ever stayed a secret for long there anyway. Middle school was pretty much the exact opposite of the CIA when it came to confidential information.

"I don't tell *everybody everything*. I never told anyone about that time you stuck your foot in the toilet in the boys' bathroom trying to hide from Carl Vanderschlot," Oz offered in his defense.

"That was you, dinglebutt."

"Oh . . . yeah," Oz mused. "Well. I never told anyone how you once ate so much spaghetti at Maglioni's that you vomited down the back of the man at the table behind you."

"You again." Bryan sighed.

"Oh . . . right. Well, don't worry about it. Because I'm here now. I will protect you."

Bryan looked at Oz's nose, already starting to turn purple from their battle in the gym, like an eggplant ripening between his eyes. "Why would I worry?" he said.

The bell rang as they ducked into social studies. Mr. Jenkins, the social studies teacher, got up from his desk and closed the door behind them. He was wearing one of his custom-made jerseys again. Mr. Jenkins operated under the delusion that historical figures should be just as popular as professional athletes, so he custom-printed baseball jerseys with the names of famous people in history—presidents, generals, dictators—and wore them to class over his button-downs. Today he was Winston Churchill, who was, apparently, number seventy-four and played for the Dodgers.

"'Success consists of going from failure to failure without loss of enthusiasm,'" Mr. Jenkins said, pointing to the same quote on the board. "Can anyone guess who said that?"

Everybody knew. The name was written on the man's shirt. Still, nobody guessed, refusing to give Jenkins the satisfaction. It was the same routine every day.

"Winston Churchill, prime minister of Great Britain during World War Two and one of the finest leaders of the twentieth century," the social studies teacher answered for them.

What followed was a seven-minute lecture on how fantastic Winston Churchill was, how he ushered his country through the most turbulent time in its history, and how he could have beaten the snot out of LeBron James in a one-on-one brawl. No one bothered to argue. No one ever bothered arguing. Bryan tried to picture Sir Winston and King James duking it out, but the image kept reverting back to scenes of Tank Wattly smashing Bryan's face into the ground. He flashed Oz a dirty look, just to let him know that he was still angry.

". . . which is why he and General Patton could have trounced the entire Cleveland Cavaliers starting lineup," the social studies teacher concluded. Old Man Jenkins waited for someone to disagree, then produced a butterscotch candy from his pocket and popped it into his mouth. "As much as I'd love to continue extolling the virtues of the British Bulldog," number seventy-four intoned, "it's Friday, so we have to finish our topography projects."

Instinctively everyone in class turned to the tables lining the back wall, on which sat a dozen misshapen spheres of various sizes. They were all supposed to be the planet Earth, though it was hard to tell with most of them. The majority had been made out of papier-mâché slapped onto balloons or rubber balls. Others had been made of tinfoil or Styrofoam. One was made entirely out of duct tape. They were all in various stages of construction. The duct tape one looked a little like the half-completed Death Star.

Bryan sighed in relief. Compared with math and gym, it looked like fifth period would be a cinch. Maybe he could get through it without seeing any mysterious messages at all. Oz tapped him from behind.

"Still mad?"

Bryan leaned back and whispered, "It's only been five minutes."

Mr. Jenkins droned on at the front of the class. "Remember, these are *topographical* representations. I want to *feel* the bumps of the mountains. I want to *see* the crevice of the Grand Canyon. I should be able to tell the difference between Death Valley and Mount Fuji."

Another tap on the shoulder. "How 'bout now?"

"*Yes*," Bryan hissed. "Still mad."

"And if I catch anyone trying to sniff the rubber cement again, I'm sending you straight down to Mr. Petrowski's office. All right. Find your groups and get started."

With a wave of his hands, the social studies teacher sent everyone to work. Oz stepped in front of Bryan, meeting him face-to-face, eyes droopy, lips in full pout. He looked ridiculous, especially with his purple nose— just how Rudolph might look, if he'd ever been caught peeing on Santa's carpet. "I hate it when you're angry," he said.

"You are the one who is going to have to notify my parents of my death," Bryan said.

"Wait a minute," Oz said, looking surprised. "You're not suggesting you're actually going to *show up* this afternoon?"

Bryan brushed past him, heading for the back table where Heather McDonald, the third member of their globe-making group, was gathering supplies.

"I'm not sure I have a choice," Bryan whispered behind him. "You heard Wattly. If I *don't* show up, he will torture me for the rest of the year."

"He's going to torture you anyway!" Oz said.

"Not if I'm dead," Bryan replied. "Come on, let's just get to work."

They scooted a few desks together, and Bryan sat down and waved across them to Heather, who barely acknowledged him with a blink. Heather McDonald was so shy she made Gina Ramirez look outgoing.

Bryan had seen her hanging out with a couple of other girls outside of class, so he knew she had friends, but in school she was the equivalent of a dormouse, squeaking only when called on and hiding in corners or behind her books.

"Hey, Heather," Oz said, finding a seat.

She made a barely audible sound. Bryan grabbed a box of toothpicks and some of the rubber cement. Their globe was one of the papier-mâché variety and nearly finished. They had all the geographical features mapped—ridges and rises for the mountains, and tiny craters for the volcanoes. Everything had been painted by Heather, who was nimble with a brush and had an eye for detail. All that was left was landmarks. It had been Bryan's idea not simply to mark them with a Sharpie, the way the other groups had done, but actually to build them and attach them to the globe, giving it an added layer of dimensionality. Mount Rushmore, the Golden Gate Bridge, the Pyramids, the Great Wall, Sydney Opera House, the Colosseum—all finished. All that was left was the toothpick Eiffel Tower and the Stonehenge made of Pez. For a moment Bryan thought maybe they would just work quietly in peace, but Oz wouldn't let up.

"You could always try to explain," he said, doing what best friends do: trying to solve a problem by offering solutions that they themselves won't be responsible for carrying out.

"What, like, write him a note?"

"Yeah, maybe."

Bryan tried to imagine what *that* might look like. *Dear Tank: Please don't murder me. I never called your mother stupid, and I only called you an ape because of your muscular build and your ferocious demeanor, not because of the abnormal carpet of back hair that is clearly visible underneath your T-shirts.* Or maybe just, *Dear Chris: Do you hate me? Or do you hate-me hate me? Please check one.* Of course this assumed that Wattly could read. Perhaps Bryan could draw a picture instead. "Maybe I should just tell him it was *your* fault," Bryan said thoughtfully.

Oz's face fell, but at least it shut him up.

"You're talking about Chris Wattly. You can just say it, you know."

Bryan turned and looked at Heather, who quickly glanced back down at her Stonehenge. It was the longest string of words he'd ever heard her tie together.

"So *you* know about me and Chris Wattly?" If Heather knew, that meant everyone knew.

Heather nodded self-consciously. "How you called him a fart-eating orangutan and said his mother was so dumb she ate twelve boxes of Wheat Thins hoping to get skinny?"

Oz snorted. Mr. Jenkins looked his way to make sure he didn't have a jar of rubber cement in his hands. Bryan gave his best friend another piercing look, then turned back to Heather. "I never said that."

Heather met his eyes. "Oh," she answered. "That's too bad."

Bryan looked at Heather McDonald—all four and a half feet of her, bangs kept long to hide her hazel eyes, tucked into a sweater a size too big, so that she looked like a turtle with an oversize shell. Heather McDonald, who had probably been teased most of her life just for being an introvert and having freckles. "Guys like that need to be brought down a peg," she added, blushing at the very idea.

Bryan finished gluing the top of the Eiffel Tower and set it aside to dry. "Not by guys like me, they don't," he said.

Heather shrugged. When she scrunched her shoulders up, her head nearly vanished inside the wool. "Do one thing every day that scares you." She placed the final candy on top of her Stonehenge cairn.

"Winston Churchill?" Bryan guessed, half jokingly.

"Eleanor Roosevelt."

"Wasn't she on the last season of *Survivor*?" Oz said, desperate to be part of the conversation.

Heather groaned and shook her head. Bryan glued the base of the Eiffel Tower in the general vicinity of France, though it was large enough to dwarf most of western Europe. Oz finished repairing a section of the Great Wall of China by regluing the LEGO that had come loose. The three of them sat back and stared at their project. It was, by far, the best in the class. Heather said it was beautiful, and Bryan said, "Yeah. It really is."

Oz reached out and fingered the top of the Play-Doh Mount Rushmore. "This must be exactly how God felt."

Bryan and Heather both looked at him funny. Then Heather carefully set the globe aside to finish drying and excused herself to go use the restroom. When she was gone, Oz and Bryan hunkered down behind their earth, away from Mr. Jenkins's sweeping gaze.

"So . . . you still mad?"

Bryan looked at Oz's dopey face, then up at the clock. He had managed to stay angry for nearly thirty minutes. It was a record. But he wasn't going to let Oz off that easy. "You owe me," he said.

Oz nodded. "I know."

"No. Literally *owe* me," Bryan continued. "You want to make me not mad at you anymore, give me some money."

Oz stopped pouting. "You're serious?"

Bryan patted his nearly empty pockets. He literally had only a cent to his name. "I've only got one coin left, and I don't know how many I'm going to need. I'm desperate." He snapped his fingers.

"This is extraction," Oz said, reaching into his own pocket.

"You mean extortion," Bryan said. "And it isn't. This is you making up for ruining my life."

Oz held his hands up, palms out. Empty.

"Nothing?" Bryan asked. Then the Wizard of Elmhurst Park reached behind Bryan's ear and produced a shiny quarter with a flourish, holding it between two fingers.

"Ta-da."

"Neat," Bryan said, pretending to be impressed by a trick he'd seen Oz perform a dozen times. "What else you got?"

Oz shrugged. "That's it, man. Sorry."

One measly quarter. That's all Bryan's forgiveness was worth. It would have to do.

"All right, people," Mr. Jenkins called. "Let's start cleaning up."

Bryan helped Oz put the supplies away, then went back to his desk, pulled his knees up, and shed the second skin of cement from the tips of his fingers. As he peeled, he thought about Jess and the time they'd spent half of art class looking at each other's fingerprints in the films of dried Elmer's. Anytime he used glue, he thought of her. And lots of other times too.

Mr. Jenkins was inspecting everyone's progress. "I see some groups still have work to do. Those of you who *are* finished, why don't you bring them up to the front and show them to the rest of the class. Bryan, it looks like your group is done." Winston Churchill motioned for someone in Bryan's group to step forward. Bryan started to get up but then thought better of it.

Not today. That would just be asking for it. He wasn't about to make himself the center of attention—again. Oz could do it. It would be part of his atonement. But as Bryan turned around, he caught Heather's eye.

Heather, who was sitting all the way in the back, closest to the table. Right next to their project. Bryan pointed at their globe and raised his eyebrows. She shook her head emphatically. Bringing things to the front of the class was not something Heather McDonald did. Not any day. Not ever. But Bryan shook his head right back at her. "El-a-nor Roos-a-velt," he mouthed. Do one thing every day that scares you.

Heather groaned, but she pushed herself out of her chair with a louder-than-usual screech and carefully picked up their monument-laden papier-mâché globe with both hands. He could see by the look in her eyes that she despised him at that moment. She made her way toward the front of the room, warily maneuvering between the aisles, careful not to bump into anyone, the planet cradled in her hands. Bryan watched with satisfaction. She might hate him now, but he knew this was good for her. Later she would appreciate it. She would tell her husband how some boy in middle school named Bryan Biggins helped pull her out of her shell, turning her into the determined, outgoing woman she was today. Bryan smiled, then looked down the aisle.

He stopped smiling.

He saw the foot a second too late to do anything about it. It was Tiffany Collins, one of the girls who sat at Missy Middleton's table at lunch, upper echelon of the pyramid. It was a sly maneuver. A no-look move so that she could plead her innocence afterward if necessary, but it was obvious to Bryan, who had been tripped enough times to know.

He watched as Heather's toe caught on Tiffany's outstretched boot. Saw one knee buckle. Saw the look of horror on Heather's pale-as-snow face, the recognition of what was happening, all too late, her loss of control. He saw her immediate future, sprawled out on the floor. Saw the two dozen fingers stabbing at the air around her, pointing and laughing. She squeaked as she fell.

Bryan watched the world spin.

And then everything slowed way down. Or it seemed to slow. Except for Bryan, who was still moving at normal speed. He practically leaped out of his chair, heading toward Heather and the world they had built together. She juggled it—the earth. Once. Twice. He saw it on her fingertips. She didn't take her eyes off of it. She was more concerned with holding on to the world than catching herself, but she just couldn't. It slipped out of her fingers and hit the desk beside her, smashing the LEGO Great Wall to pieces. The earth bounced once, still in slow motion, as if time itself were drawing to an end. The Eiffel Tower splintered and collapsed. It was Armageddon.

Bryan dodged between chairs, between the seats of his wide-eyed classmates, watching the earth roll forward to the edge of the desk, none of them bothering to stop it. They were bystanders, half of them observing the globe roll toward its doom, the other half staring at the body of Heather McDonald spread across the floor. Even Mr. Jenkins stood there, unmoving.

The earth hit the edge of the desk.

Bryan leaped over Heather's prone body.

The world plummeted.

He dived. Arms outstretched. Chest and knees and elbows slamming into the cold, dusty cement floor, knocking the wind out of him. Reaching. Reaching. *Reaching.*

He felt it. Dropping into his palms, the paint still tacky in places, the fingers of one hand knocking over the Great Pyramid. Yet he held on, even as he hit the floor, even as the air was ripped out of him, not daring to take his eyes off of it. The whole world in his hands.

Everything sped back up again.

Bryan shook away the dizziness and chanced a look around. At his classmates, who all stared back at him. At Mr. Churchill-Jenkins, whose own hands were clasped over his heart. At Tiffany, swiftly pulling her foot back under her desk but scowling at him as she did.

At Heather McDonald. Who lay on the ground beside him. Who, for some reason, was not being laughed at, despite the fact that she had gone down like the *Titanic*. Who looked at him with a strange gleam in her eyes, as if he had just saved her life.

And at Oz, who was finally out of his chair, well after the fact, and was crouched next to them.

"Dude," he said, staring at Bryan, his voice couched in awe. "You did it. You actually did it."

He pointed to the globe, mostly intact, nestled in Bryan's grip.

"You actually saved the world."

1:30 P.M.
THE BEAST IN THE DARKNESS

↓

FIFTY XP.

That's how many experience points you get for saving the world. The equivalent of reading aloud a scene of Shakespeare. Fifty experience points. And he hadn't even leveled up.

"Seems kind of cheap," Oz said when Bryan told him about the words he saw arcing above their papier-mâché globe at the end of social studies. The same color as always, hovering right over Earth like a vibrant blue cloud.

+50 XP.

Much better than the experience points, at least,

was the mumbled thank-you from Heather, who then turned and shot daggers at Tiffany Collins, who rolled her eyes right back.

Bryan's knees and elbows hurt from the landing. He had jarred his teeth slamming into the floor. Who said saving the world would be easy? He walked with Oz through the halls.

"So that wasn't it, then. Saving the world," Oz wondered. "That wasn't enough?"

"I don't think that was it." Fifty experience points was good and all, but keeping their social studies project from smashing on the floor wasn't what he was destined to do, apparently. It was a side quest, if anything. A lucky catch. The game wasn't over. Bryan would know when it was over. He didn't know *how* he would know, but he would know.

"So there's still something left, right? Something big? Something important?" Oz prodded.

Bryan knew what his friend was thinking. He knew because Bryan had been thinking the same thing. All through fifth period. Ever since he'd left the cafeteria. They stopped in the hall outside of Bryan's next class, the last one before band.

"It's him." Bryan didn't even have to say his name. "I *have* to face him."

Oz nodded. "The Demon King," he whispered.

"The Sovereign of Darkness."

"It makes perfect sense," Oz said.

Bryan shot Oz a dirty look.

"I mean, in its own completely messed-up way it makes sense. Sort of."

He was right. There was a certain insane logic to it. All of this had to be building to something. A final confrontation. Bryan checked the time on his phone. He had less than two and a half hours left till his rendezvous with Tank.

"And what happens if you don't meet him?" Oz asked. "Do you lose?"

Suddenly Bryan didn't see any way he could win. "I don't know."

"Don't worry," Oz said, putting both hands on Bryan's shoulders. "We'll think of something. Just make it through . . . what do you have left?"

"Science," Bryan muttered.

He could tell Oz wanted to say, *What could possibly go wrong in science?* Except Myra had said the same thing about social studies. So he just kept his mouth shut and gave Bryan's shoulders a squeeze. "Hang in there," was all he could offer.

Bryan watched Oz go, gently prodding at his purple nose. In the room, Mr. Tomlins, the science teacher, was bent over one of the lab tables, messing with something underneath. The other kids were all seated already, whispering to one another. One of them, Vanessa, who had been sitting next to Tiffany in social studies, pointed at Bryan and smirked. Everyone else at her table laughed. He couldn't imagine the kinds of things that were being said about him behind his back today.

Mr. Tomlins motioned for everyone to be quiet as Bryan found his seat by the door. Tomlins was wearing his lab coat today. Not a good sign. Bryan had been hoping they would just watch a video or something, anything to keep him out of trouble, but lab coat meant hands-on learning, which even on a normal day usually meant disaster.

"Today we are going to continue our discussion of behavioral science—specifically the idea of conditioning: training your brain to respond a certain way to outside stimuli." Bryan watched Mr. Tomlins pace back and forth behind his giant granite-topped desk in the front of the room. The man was short—barely over five feet—and wore thin glasses that seemed to get lost on his wide red face. His balding forehead glared in the overhead lights. He reminded Bryan a little of that Muppet—the puffy-faced science guy with glasses but no eyeballs on his melon head.

"For example, the next time that bell rings, all of you will immediately forget everything I've told you. You will scramble for your backpacks, and you will rush out that door without so much as a simple thank-you for all the mind-blowing knowledge I bestowed upon you today. You will do so mindlessly, as you have for the last several weeks of school, because it is a *conditioned* response. The bell is a stimulus and you are conditioned to act a certain way when you hear it."

Like ducking behind someone taller as soon as you spot Tank Wattly coming down the hall, Bryan thought. *Or losing your ability to say anything witty or intelligent whenever this one girl in particular so much as looks at you.*

"We are all conditioned by our environment. We are all creatures of instinct, driven by our need to survive, but capable of learning through experience. In that way we are actually no different," Tomlins said, reaching beneath him and pulling up a wire cage from under the table, "from mice."

Susan Onesacker screamed, but the rest of the class bent forward to get a better look at the tufts of white fur huddled against one another in the cage. There had to be at least a dozen of them in there. Beady little red eyes. Twitching noses. Some of the mice lifted their snouts to the air. Others started clawing to find an exit. They didn't look that smart. Of course, neither did half the people in the room as far as Bryan was concerned.

Bryan moaned softly to himself. He didn't like where this was going at all.

"You're going to give us rabies," Kaitlin Spencer said.

"My religion forbids me from dissecting animals," Alisha Patel said.

"Do we get to electrocute them?"

Mr. Tomlins shook his head emphatically.

"No, you are *not* electrocuting them, Jordan. Or dissecting them. They are just ordinary mice, and they are probably cleaner than you are, Ms. Spencer."

"Probably cleaner than Miner, anyway," someone whispered. Bryan looked over at Charlie, who was sitting at a lab table by himself. He either hadn't heard or was pretending not to. Any other day Bryan would have felt bad for him, but today he had his own problems. Mr. Tomlins shot a disapproving look in the direction of the comment, then turned his attention back to the cage.

"These mice are hardly dangerous; however, they must be handled with care." Tomlins poked a pinkie between the slats of the cage, earning a sniff from one of the more inquisitive rodents. "Now if you look under your tables, you will find a kit containing a plastic baseboard and several walls. Your first job is to follow the instructions and build the maze. I will come around and pass out the other materials you will need for your experiment. Be sure to have your lab journals out as well, as you will need to record your data. Once your mazes are finished, I will come by and give each table its test subject."

"So disgusting," the girl sitting across from Bryan whispered, but Bryan just ignored her. He didn't reach beneath the table for the maze or get out his lab

JOHN DAVID ANDERSON

journal either. He just watched the cage full of mice, waiting, counting down in his head.

Because he knew it was coming. That was just how the day was shaping up. He had been conditioned to expect the worst.

He didn't have to wait long.

It was sheer clumsiness. An accident. Or maybe not. Bryan didn't know anymore. Mr. Tomlins, giving directions, holding the cage in one hand, swung it around and knocked it against the edge of the table. Just hard enough to cause two of the latches to pop and the plastic bottom of the cage to come loose, dumping a pile of mulch on the floor. The science teacher's knees buckled as he bent low to slam the thing back together, but not in time. Four of the mice tumbled out through the opening, landing in the mulch pile, and were now scurrying in four different directions, making a break for it. Free at last.

"Oh jeez!" Mr. Tomlins cursed, fumbling to put the cage back together and ensure no more critters escaped.

Susan Onesacker screamed again, but this time she was joined by several others. Students jumped up on top of their chairs or tables. Micah Parker—who everyone knew owned a small petting zoo in his house, including seven cats and a boa constrictor—immediately started chasing after one of the escaped rodents, cooing at it to "come here and be still."

"Don't just stand there, help me!" Mr. Tomlins roared. The science teacher was on his hands and knees now, trying to corner another escapee. Bryan leaped to his feet and followed a flash of white. The mice were surprisingly fast. One ran over Kaitlin's foot, causing her to swoon, crashing into Tamara Brown, who barely caught her. Bryan heard the sound of foot stomps and looked to see Jordan trying to smash one under his heel.

"Stop it!" Tomlins yelled. "No stomping! Your orders are to capture only!"

It was chaos. Chairs were flipped. Bags were emptied to try and make traps. The science teacher upended a wastebasket, dumping the trash right onto the floor, then used it to ensnare one of the mice. Bryan watched as Micah scooped another into his hands, whispering to it softly. There were only two left.

A flash of white darted across the floor right past Bryan's shoe, headed toward the door, which

Mr. Tomlins had at least had the sense to close before class started.

"Come here, you little fuzz ball," Bryan said. He dropped to his knees and reached out to grab it by the tail. Then stopped as the door swung open. Becky Yao stood there, a blue hall pass in her hand.

"Sorry, Mr. Tomlins, but I had to stay after and talk to Mrs. Bedfer—*what the* . . . ?" She looked down just as the mouse scurried between her legs and out into the hall.

Bryan leaped to his feet. Turned and looked at Mr. Tomlins.

"Go!" the science teacher shouted.

Bryan pushed past Becky into the hall. Behind him he could hear the continued screams of Susan Onesacker and the words of Mr. Tomlins calling out to him. "Remember, Biggins, I want him alive!"

Bryan stopped long enough to slam the door shut behind him. He looked for a wisp of movement, listened for a squeak or the patter of paws, but it was impossible to hear anything with all the commotion from the room behind him. Bryan started to turn to go one way when a ball of white fuzz ambled out from behind a water fountain and darted the other way. Bryan took off after it.

"Come here, you little rat." He lunged, trying to cut it off, but the mouse slipped by him, its little paws struggling to find traction on the slick tiled floor. Bryan was nearly on top of it again as the mouse turned the corner at the end of the hall.

He turned to see the beast taking cover under an empty desk sitting in the hallway. It was huddled against the wall. He had it trapped. He had to be stealthy, though. It would be easier if he had Kerran Nightstalker's Shroud of Invisibility rather than his own sweat-stained Tunic of Unwashing, but he could at least walk on his tiptoes, holding his breath. Just creep . . . right . . . up . . . on . . . it . . . like . . . Mercutio . . . the . . . ninja . . . and . . .

"Biggins!"

Bryan froze at the sound of the voice shouting his name.

He knew that voice.

He slowly turned his head.

There she was, at the end of the hall, standing stiff as a surfboard. Eyes black as midnight, amplified by her thick lenses.

The Eye of Krug sees all.

Bryan kept his own eyes on the mouse as she approached, her leather soles clopping steadily down the hallway. "I sure hope you have a hall pass this time," she demanded, stopping in front of Bryan and holding out her hand.

"I don't, actually," Bryan whispered through clenched teeth. "See, I'm on a mission from Mr. Tomlins." He tried to motion toward the mouse with his thumb, but Amy wasn't taking the hint. Instead she snapped her fingers in front of his face to get his full attention. Bryan thought she could be cute if she wasn't snarling all the time.

"Look at me, Biggins. Don't you know that you aren't allowed to wander the halls without a pass *officially* signed by a teacher or administrator?"

"Is this, like, your full-time job or something?" Bryan fired back. "I told you I'm out here helping Mr. Tomlins."

The Eye ignored Bryan's question. Her eyebrows made a sharp V, like a dagger's tip. "Obedience to the law is demanded as a right; not asked as a favor," she said.

"Why do people keep *quoting* things at me?" Bryan blustered. "What does that even *mean*?"

"It means show me your hall pass or I'm writing you up!" Krug snapped her fingers at him again. Bryan noticed her nails were cut to the quick.

"And I told *you*," he repeated, speaking slowly this time, looking into her cold, calculating eyes, "I . . . don't . . . *have* . . . a . . . pass. I am on a mission to capture a mouse that escaped from Mr. Tomlins's class and is sitting right . . . over . . ." He pointed behind him to where the mouse was, except, of course, the mouse was already gone. "Terrific. You let it get away."

Bryan felt one of Amy's hands on his arm. "That's it, Biggins. That's the second time you've been out of class today. I'm taking you in to see the Boss."

The Boss. The principal. Mr. Petrowski. Bryan started to plead his case, when he saw the little white fuzz ball dart back across the hall.

"There it is!" he shouted, and started after it, but Amy's hands clamped down. The Eye of Krug was holding him back. He jerked his arm free, but she grabbed him by both shoulders. She was a lot stronger than she looked. "Get off of me!" he yelled.

"No! You're going to the principal's office!" she grunted.

He tried to wiggle out of her grasp, but instead she wrapped her arms tightly around his chest and then jumped up and knotted her legs around his waist, suddenly riding him piggyback. The whole maneuver threw him off balance, causing them both to spin around twice and then topple over onto the floor in a heap of grunts and flailing limbs. Bryan heard an "urf" from beneath him and felt Amy's grip loosen around his neck. He pried himself free and scrambled back to his feet.

He looked down to see her holding her stomach, eyes clenched tight, the wind knocked out of her. She opened her eyes and glared at him, but somehow her suit jacket had gotten twisted around her, making it difficult for her to move her arms to get up. She actually growled. Like a wild animal.

"Seriously, Amy, I'm sorry, but you have to understand," Bryan said, then saw the mouse turn another corner. Before she could get up and follow, Bryan took off down the hall. Behind him he could hear her voice.

"This isn't over Biggins! You're in big trouble now!"

Tell me something I don't know, he thought, running in the same direction as the mouse. He had to catch it. He wasn't sure how many continues he had left.

Bryan turned just in time to see the mouse duck through the crack of a barely opened door, leading into another room that Bryan had never been in before.

The boiler room.

"You've got to be joking."

The thing might as well have gone into the kitchen. Or out into the field behind the school. Bryan stood outside the cracked door and looked back down the hall, expecting to see Amy right there, shambling after him, but there was nobody. Maybe she was headed to the front office. If so, Bryan knew he would need evidence to support his story. He would have to catch this little rodent. Bryan pushed open the door to the boiler room and squeezed inside.

The long hall of a room was dark and musty, floors of cold cement, a maze of pipes and ducts crossing and bending and disappearing into the ceiling. Furnaces and hot-water heaters lined up like high-rise apartments, shooting metal tubes and hoses out in all

JOHN DAVID ANDERSON

directions. Valves hissed. Generators hummed. The whole place smelled of burned oil and pine cleaner. There were at least a million places a mouse could hide in here.

"Impossible," Bryan said to himself.

"Nouthin's impossible."

Bryan jumped, spinning to see Mr. McKellen, the school's head janitor, standing right beside him. It certainly wasn't the first time Bryan had seen the man, but it *was* the first time he'd heard him speak. The head janitor was at least eighty years old, by the look of him, with an avalanche of a beard that came halfway down his shirt and eyes ringed with crags and crevices. He had oily rags poking out of both pockets and an assortment of screwdrivers clipped to his belt. He looked at Bryan with one bushy eyebrow raised. "Ya dunna balong here, ya know?" the old man said.

"I know. I'm sorry," Bryan said. Did the man *always* have an accent or was that only for today? Bryan wondered. The janitor's eyes were a cloudy blue. It was a little unsettling, bewitching even. Like the old man could see into the future or something. "I was chasing a mouse," Bryan explained. "White. About yay big.

Pink tail. It escaped from Mr. Tomlin's class and came in here."

The janitor nodded, stroked his long beard. "I know this creature a which ya speak," he said, chewing on each word as if it were stuck to the roof of his mouth. "A cunnin' thing. And vicious."

Bryan shook his head. "No. I'm just looking for a mouse, see? It got free from—"

"Cunnin' and vicious!" the janitor insisted, blowing up those ominous eyes and advancing on Bryan with his hands up. "With claws lek deggers and teeth sharp enoof to dig clane through a man's heart and out t'other side!" Mr. McKellen reached out with both hands. Bryan instinctively backed up against the wall. The janitor smiled, and Bryan saw he was missing more than one tooth.

"Sartin we've seen their kind bafore. Tried everythin'. Poison. Metal. Wire. All manner a traps. But they're wily beasts. Once heard a oon got clar in ta the lounge. Hid in the cabinet till the music teacher came and joomped right at 'er; nearly ripped 'er face off, it did."

"I really don't think—" Bryan started to say, but the old man cut him off.

"Ever been par'lyzed with fear, Mr. Biggins?"

"Wait a minute. How do you know who I—"

"Ever felt the ice-cold tooch a death wrap its bony fingers round yer neck?"

"No, but—"

"Ever know what it's like to stare inta those beady red eyes and know ya only have one breath left ta yer name?"

This old man was seriously creeping Bryan out.

"Such is the demon ya seek." The old janitor coughed. Then he laughed. A full-throated, rasping laugh, making the loose skin of his cheeks jump.

"*The demon*," Bryan whispered to himself, looking down at his shoes and then back up at the janitor. "Right, okay. Listen, Mr. McKellen, I'm just going to look around a little bit, you know, just to say I tried. If you want to help—"

"Do ya take me fer a fool, Biggins?" the janitor interrupted. "I'm sure as sin not goin' after that 'orrible creature. Best I kin do is ta give ya *this*." The janitor reached behind him and handed Bryan a broom. Not one of the broad-headed sweepers that look like giant mustaches and span half a hallway, but a normal kitchen broom that seemed to be missing half of its bristles.

"Wow. Um. Okay. Thanks . . . for this," Bryan said, taking it tentatively.

"Don't joodge it by its looks. The Staff a Sweeping Joostice has been among our kin for decades. My great-grandfather used it. My own father wielded it. Now you'll carry it, Bryan Biggins. Into the darkness that awaits ya."

"Okay. Whatever. Listen: If a crazy girl in a black business suit and glasses comes to the door looking for me, just tell her I'm not here, all right?" Bryan turned to start looking, but the janitor stopped him again with a hand on his shoulder.

"Be on yer guard, Biggins. There're even fouler thin's than your moose hidden in these shadows."

Right. Bryan nodded. *My moose.* "Got it," he said, then he took the broom and ventured deeper into the boiler room. He had taken about ten steps when he heard the door slam shut and turned to see that the old janitor with the ghost-blue eyes was gone. He was on his own in this wasteland of steaming machines and empty crates.

JOHN DAVID ANDERSON

He had the overwhelming sensation that he'd done something like this before. It was really no different from most of the dungeons he'd conquered in Sovereign of Darkness. Except in those he'd *used* a mouse to fend off evil with a click of his finger. He hadn't been *looking* for one. Not to mention Kerran Nightstalker was usually armed with a sword and a bow, not an ancient broom.

Bryan ventured deeper into the room. Half the lights were burned out, creating patches of darkness. Spare piping and random hunks of metal littered the floor. Bryan took small steps, craning his neck, looking into every crack and crevice. Listening. He thought he could hear a scratching. Soft at first, but growing louder. Tiny claws scraping along metal. It seemed to echo almost, so that Bryan couldn't really tell where it was coming from. Everywhere and nowhere. All around. He gripped his broom tighter in both hands.

Cunnin' and vicious. The janitor's words whispered in his head. The mouse—half the size of Bryan's fist—hadn't looked either when Bryan was chasing it down the hall, but suddenly he wasn't so sure. He could sense it there, somewhere close by, watching him. Waiting.

A shadow danced along the far wall, the silhouette of a mouse, except ten times larger than the one Bryan had been hunting. Bryan held the Staff of Sweeping Justice out in front of him, thinking of a horror movie he had seen once where the kid flushed a baby alligator down the toilet and it somehow found enough to eat in the sewers to grow twelve feet long, eventually crawling through a manhole to terrorize the town. Bryan pictured the mouse, suddenly three feet tall, with front teeth like razor blades and claws like kitchen knives capable of tearing through skin and bone, looming up behind him.

Something knocked and rattled. Bryan spun around and struck at whatever it was with his broom, hitting the furnace that had just kicked on, making an obnoxious gonging sound. A blower or fan suddenly whirred to life.

Bryan shook his head. He had to get a hold of himself. He was after a mouse. Nothing more.

He felt something rub against his leg.

"Aaaaagggghhh!"

He whirled around, sweeping out with the business end of his broom, doing untold damage to a

JOHN DAVID ANDERSON

pocket of cobwebs and banging against a pipe, feeling the tremor dance back up his arms and down his spine. Bryan looked all over the floor, spinning in circles. Something had touched him. Something had run by. He was sure of it. He couldn't see anything, though, only the shadows on the wall. He spun around, broom held like a battle-ax, trying to catch his breath. *Calm down, Bryan. It's just your imagination. There's nothing else in here but you and that stupid mouse.*

He paused. Listened.

Then he felt it. On top of his head. Falling. Dropping. *Crawling.*

It was in his hair.

"Gyyaaaaahhh!"

He dropped the broom and shook his head frantically, batting at it with both hands, seeing whatever it was hit the floor. He banged his left hand hard against an overhead duct and saw a red flash.

-2 HP.

Bryan stuffed his three pulsing fingers into his mouth and looked down, blinking away tears. There, on the gray cement slab of the floor, was a spider, or what was left of it, the thing that had dropped into his hair.

Just to be sure, Bryan picked up the Staff of Sweeping Justice and gave it a follow-up smash, smearing its guts across the floor.

+10 XP.

There're even fouler thin's than your moose hidden in these shadows. Guess so. Bryan wasn't a huge fan of spiders. Much worse than mice, though not nearly as frightening as Tanks.

Another sound—some other machine roaring to life or some other hideous creature growling behind him. Bryan stepped back instinctively, tripping over a drainpipe, and then stumbled, falling against a water heater, arms flailing. He heard something snap and felt a sharp pain in his left buttock. More red letters appeared in the air before him.

-3 HP.

He looked down.

"Oh no."

Beneath him was the Staff of Sweeping Justice, splintered in two where he had landed on it. He pulled the two pieces free and held them together, assessing the damage, then rubbed the sore spot on his butt where the splintered ends had jabbed him.

It was hopeless. He was never going to find that mouse, and likely he would kill himself or blow up the school trying. He looked back in the direction of the door. He should give up before he broke something even more precious than Mr. McKellen's broom. He started to get up, when he heard the scratching again. Saw the shadow, even larger this time, almost twice the size of his head. It was growing somehow, becoming gigantic. The shadow moved along the wall. Coming closer. Closer still.

Coming straight for him, in fact.

Bryan held on to the top half of the splintered broom, wielding it like a stake, ready to stab the beast as it lunged for him, hoping to find its evil heart before it could go for his throat.

"I'm not afraid of you!" Bryan shouted at the shadow.

The creature let out a terrible squeak as it appeared from behind a bucket.

All three inches of it.

Its nose sniffed the air questioningly. Bryan sighed.

It hadn't grown. It wasn't a monster. It was barely bigger than a walnut, though it did stare at Bryan with its piercing fiery-red eyes. The mouse bared its

INSERT COIN TO CONTINUE

teeth and nibbled at the air. Bryan bared his own teeth back.

"Not so vicious after all, are you?" he said.

He looked around. The way he was sitting with his front legs spread, there wasn't much place for the rodent to go. If he could just stretch out his feet on either side, he could box it off with only the bucket for it to hide behind. He had it trapped.

The mouse stared at Bryan, who slowly reached for the other half of the broom, the one with the bristles. He held it up before him, resting the bottom of the shaft on the cement slab.

"You. Shall. Not. Pass," he said.

The mouse sniffed the air. Then lowered its head.

And came straight for him.

Straight for one leg, in fact, and the inviting opening in the cuff of Bryan's jeans. Before he could think of what to do, the creature had scampered up past his Boot of Average Walking Speed and burrowed beneath his Breeches of Enduring Stiffness, little claws scrabbling along Bryan's bare skin, crawling steadily upward along his leg.

Bryan shrieked. He could feel it, tickling and scratching all at once, as the rodent tunneled its way up his pants, up to his knee, toward his boxers. He squirmed and grabbed hold of a nearby pipe and pulled himself to his feet as quickly as he could, kicking out with the one leg as he did. He felt the little ball of fur slide along his leg, shooting out of the cuff of his pants in an arc. Curving high into the air.

Landing right in the bucket with a *thunk*.

Bryan stood there for a moment, paralyzed, the thought of the mouse nearly reaching his underwear. Then he recovered enough to pull his pant leg up and inspect for damage. There was a barely visible scratch. No bites. No rabies. No bubonic plague. Not even a lost hit point. He pulled his jeans back down and looked over at the bucket. It wasn't moving. He couldn't hear anything.

"Oh no," he said again.

He got to his hands and knees and crawled over, afraid to look inside. What if he'd really killed it? A spider was one thing, but a mouse? Even one as cunning as this one. Bryan peered over the lip of the bucket.

Two beady eyes glanced up at him, a set of whiskers trembling.

The mouse was alive. It was chewing on its own foot, but it was alive. A little brain damaged, perhaps, but that was all right. He could deal with that.

He picked the bucket up by its handle and limped back toward the door, his butt cheeks still sore from sitting on the broom. He stooped to pick up the two pieces of the Staff of Sweeping Justice, holding them in one hand, the trapped mouse in the other.

The door to the boiler room was open, but Mr. McKellen was nowhere to be seen. Bryan left the remnants of the staff with the other mops and brooms, thinking he would have to find the man and apologize at some point. Then he readjusted his grip on the handle of the bucket and stepped out into the hall cautiously, scanning in all directions. The coast was clear.

Beware the Eye of Krug.

The Eye of Krug sees everything. But maybe Bryan's falling on top of her had knocked Amy out of commission for the afternoon. Bryan started past the door that led out to the track and the football field, heading back toward Mr. Tomlins's room in B Hall, ready to collect on his bounty. *How many experience points do you earn for capturing an escaped rodent?* he wondered. Surely as much as saving the world. He smiled at his small victory, his step shifting from mope to saunter, when something in the back-door window caught his eye.

Someone was out there. Standing outside in the rain. Jess.

Standing under the eaves, just out of the downpour, in fact, leaning against the brick wall. Her hands were stuffed deep into her jeans. Head hung, hair in her eyes. She looked to be alone, framed by the dark gray clouds.

Bryan never saw Jess alone. She wasn't like Missy, always swarmed by a gaggle of fawning groupies, but she wasn't like Myra, either, tucked into a corner with her sketchbook or her iPod, looking at everyone else as if they were bugs trapped behind glass. She was always with *someone*. People attached themselves to her as she walked down the hall, magnetically it seemed. And yet there she was, standing outside in the rain, all by herself.

Bryan set the bucket down, forgetting the mouse and his mission for the moment. He took a step toward the door, when someone else passed by the window.

He could just make out the back of the jacket, the

blue and gold of the Mount Comfort Lions. The gilded hair and perfect smile. Landon Prince turned so that he was looking right at her and said something. Bryan couldn't hear a word through the heavy door, but he could see enough. Jess shrugged and Landon threw his arms up in the air, then pointed to himself. Jess shook her head. Then mouthed one word.

"Bryan!"

Bryan turned, jolted back by Mr. Tomlins's voice, the science teacher shuffling down the hall, lips pursed, eyes glancing nervously from Bryan to the bucket by his feet.

"Did you . . . ? Please say you didn't . . . Is he . . . ?" The science teacher couldn't bear to say it. Bryan bent over and tipped the bucket just enough that the science teacher could see the mouse scrabbling around inside. Tomlins's face broke into a smile. He clapped his hands. "You found him. You found Mr. Mouskerson." Mr. Tomlins grabbed the bucket and stuck his hand in, stroking the top of the mouse's head. Bryan watched as the science teacher scooped the rodent up and held him close to his face. The two just rubbed noses and squeaked at each other, then

Mr. Tomlins hastily set the mouse back in the bucket.

"You did an excellent job, my boy. Excellent job. I'm not sure how I can repay you."

Bryan looked at the letters already forming above Mr. Tomlins's head.

+1ØØ XP.

LEVEL UP.

"We'll call it even," Bryan said.

Mr. Tomlins looked down at the mouse, still circling the bottom of the bucket, now trying to eat its tail. The science teacher nodded. "If you say so. But if you ever forget your homework, just let me know and we can work something out." The science teacher stuffed his face back into the bucket. "We should get you back to class, Mr. Mouskerson. Your brothers and sisters are worried *sick*."

Bryan watched Mr. Tomlins go, knowing he should follow, that he should go back to the science room and finish what was left of sixth period; instead he turned back to the door, hoping to find her still standing there, but alone this time. For-real alone. Hoping, maybe, that Landon Prince had stormed off in disappointment. That she had vanquished him.

Then Bryan would stick his head out the door and ask if she was okay. If she was cold. If she wanted to talk. And he would walk out there, a hero, and offer to put his arm around her and keep her warm.

He pressed his face up against the window and looked out across the wet pavement and into the angry gray sky. Jess was already gone.

2:24 P.M.
BAND HERO

BY THE TIME ALL THE RODENTS HAD BEEN accounted for, the furniture had been turned upright, and everyone calmed down, sixth period was nearly over. Mr. Tomlins gave the class ten minutes of free time, though most people used it to talk about the Great Mouse Escape. Kaitlin Spencer sat with her head on her knees, complaining about how she was going to sue the entire school district for negligence and emotional trauma. Micah Parker just stared at the cage, talking to the mice.

Bryan sat by himself and thought about last night

and the game and the choice he had made. All the choices he had made. He tried to piece it all together. But no matter how hard he puzzled, he couldn't help but come back to Tank and their imminent confrontation. None of the rest of it seemed to matter, or if it did, it was all obviously just building to that moment. Bryan looked up at the clock. He had less than two hours now.

The bell signifying the end of sixth period rang, and Bryan watched everyone mindlessly gather their things and head off to their last class of the day, just as Mr. Tomlins had predicted. Most of them were smiling, chatting, carefree. They could feel the freedom of the weekend already. Two days of rock concerts and basement get-togethers and hours spent sucked into their phones. As they passed, some of them looked at Bryan. Some of the looks were sympathetic, but most of them said, simply, *So glad I'm not you.*

They all knew.

Bryan grabbed his pack. He needed to get to band in time to talk to Oz and Myra. On the way to C Hall he tried to stay inconspicuous. It wasn't just Wattly he wanted to avoid. Krug was on the list now. And Mr. McKellen, who might say something about his broom.

And Reese Hawthorne, who might give Bryan a shove just because he caught that ball in gym class. And Mrs. Baylor-Tore, because she was just plain scary and he'd taken one of her Twinkies. He melted into the crowd and made it to the practice room to find Myra and Oz already waiting for him.

"Heard about the mouse," Myra said.

Bryan shook his head in disbelief. "That's impossible. That happened, like, ten minutes ago!"

"Chris P. texted Rachel, who texted me," Oz explained. "I texted Myra."

"I didn't text anybody," Myra said. "I don't like people that much."

Bryan wondered what kind of slack-off classes his friends were in that they could get away with texting each other. The one time this year he'd tried to take his phone out during class just to *read* a message, Tennenbaum had confiscated it for the whole day.

"So. What happened? Did you level up again?"

"For all the good it did," Bryan replied. "Do you guys know what happened between Jess and Landon Prince? I saw them standing outside last period. She didn't look happy." Or maybe he had just imagined her looking unhappy. He was having a hard enough time with reality as it was.

Oz's eyebrows clinched. "Seriously? You've got a fight with a fart-eating Neanderthal scheduled in less than two hours, and you're worried about what Jess Alcorn and Landon Prince are doing?"

"I never said he ate farts. That's not even physically possible." Bryan looked at Myra for confirmation. She shook her head.

"I just think we need to focus on the problem at hand, namely your insanity and impending death," Oz said. "I sent an e-mail to the creators of Sovereign of Darkness."

"You did what?" Bryan said too loudly, though so many people were tuning their instruments in the practice room it was hard to hear much of anything.

"Well. You said the game freaked out on you and deep-fried your computer and you woke up this morning and all this crazy stuff started happening, right? So I thought I'd ask them about it. See if they knew anything. Maybe they are the ones responsible."

Bryan shook his head. "Wait. So you asked them if they wrote a computer program designed to hack into my *life*?"

Oz shook his head. "I didn't put it like *that*. I just said something about a secret level at the end and asked them if they had any advice for beating it."

Bryan shrugged. He would never have thought of that. It didn't make any sense, but neither did most of what had happened today. "And did you get a response?"

"Just an automated reply saying that they care so much about me and will get to me in the next twenty-four hours."

Bryan put a hand on Oz's shoulder. "It was a thought." Not a great one, but with Oz you really had to count the thoughts or you often didn't have anything.

"So what are you going to do about Tank?" Myra asked. She looked really concerned. As if she genuinely feared for Bryan's life, which didn't make him feel any better.

"I don't know yet," Bryan said. "Though I'm not sure what choice I have."

"Well, there's no shame in running from a fight that you didn't start and can't possibly win," she said.

"Thanks for the vote of confidence."

He followed the other two into the band locker

room and pulled his saxophone from its case. He had been playing for only two months, but in that time he had progressed from what his father called "cat beaten with cactus" to "cat kicked with steel-toed boot." His mother thought he played beautifully. Personally, he thought the whole band sounded like animals being tortured. Except Myra. She was a drummer and was actually pretty good. Oz played trombone. He was awful.

They joined the other forty or so members of the school band and waited for Mr. Thorntonberry to arrive. He was running late today. Class was supposed to have started five minutes ago.

Mikey Gerard, one of the two other saxophonists, leaned over and whispered to Bryan.

"So what are you going to do?"

"Why does everybody keep asking me that?" Bryan growled.

"Just wondering. I've got two bucks says you'll show up."

Terrific. Now his classmates were taking bets. "Two whole bucks?" Bryan said.

"At ten-to-one odds," Mikey added enthusiastically.

"He's not going to show," Oz whispered from the row behind them.

"I don't know *what* I'm going to do," Bryan said again.

"Yes you do," Oz insisted. "What is there to think about? Tank will crush you."

"Between you and Myra it's a wonder I bother having friends at all."

"We only say it because we care," Oz insisted.

"You don't have to win," Mikey informed him. "Just show up. I'll split the money with you. It only seems fair."

"Great," Bryan said, wondering if ten bucks would be enough to buy a new face after Chris Wattly smeared his across the cement.

Finally Mr. Thorntonberry rushed into the practice room in his pressed slacks and sparkling vest, a sheaf of papers in hand. "Sorry, Charlies," he said, huffing. "The copier was giving me fits. Apparently, Ms. Wang is on a diet again, which always puts her in a bad mood, so she tried to put her foot through it." Mr. Thorntonberry had a fondness for drama. And sequins.

"Guess she didn't get the Twinkie after all," Oz whispered to Bryan's back.

Mr. Thorntonberry moved around the room, handing out sheet music. "We are starting a new piece today. It's fabulous, but a little beyond our level. It has a couple of short solos in it, so some of you will get the chance to *shine*." Mr. Thorntonberry made shimmery movements with his fingers, something he'd carried over from his brief, six-month stint on Broadway. Bryan took his sheet music and handed the rest down the row. The new piece was called *Overture to a Dream*. It looked really long and complicated.

"Of course, there's bets on everything," Mikey continued. "If there will be blood. If he stuffs you in the Dumpster. If they have to call an ambulance."

"An ambulance? Are you serious?" Bryan asked.

"Three-to-one odds," Mikey added.

Suddenly all faces turned frontward as Mr. Thorntonberry mounted the podium, tapping on it with his baton. "All right, people. This is our first time through, so just try to keep up. You're going to miss a few notes, but I just want to see how we do, all right? Remember: The band plays on."

"Fifty-fifty," Mikey whispered out the side of his mouth. "That's ten bucks just for showing."

"I can do the math," Bryan said, giving Mikey the meanest look he could muster, then he brought his saxophone to his lips.

Mr. Thorntonberry stood at the podium and adjusted his vest. There was a hush, a hesitation, then the music teacher snapped his fingers above his head.

Suddenly all the overhead lights went out save for a single row across the middle and a solitary lamp that beamed up from the podium, giving the bandleader an otherworldly aura, his face half illuminated, the sequins on his vest making patterns on the wall. Bryan moaned softly to himself. The band started to whisper, putting their instruments down and wondering if they had just experienced a power outage, when three sharp taps rang against the podium.

"Helllloooooo, Mount Comfort Middle School!" Mr. Thorntonberry shouted.

Silence. Everyone stared at their crazy band teacher's glowing face. Finally one of the drummers said, "Um. Hey there, Mr. T." There was a smattering of giggles.

"Are you ready to rock?" the music teacher asked.

Everyone looked at one another, though it was kind

of hard to see faces in the near darkness. Not that you needed to. This was middle school band. They mostly played Sousa. Rocking was never part of the equation, though today, it seemed, Mr. Thorntonberry had other ideas.

Then Bryan realized what was happening. *He* was doing this. This was all his fault again. Just like gym class. Just like Shakespeare. Just like everything.

"I said, are you ready to *rock*?" Thorntonberry cried out again.

"I am *so* ready," Naveen Ranjin said, putting his clarinet to his lips, clearly pumped.

"Then let's blow the roof offa this place!"

Mr. Thorntonberry thrust both hands up into the air as all the lights suddenly came back up again, burning Bryan's eyes.

"One, two, three, four . . ."

Thorntonberry brought his hands down and the band suddenly launched into a flurry of notes. It was an explosion of sound, discordant and shrieking, like opening the doors to a cat-kicking *convention*, and Bryan felt a chill work its way all along his spine. He would have plugged his ears except he was too busy fingering wrong notes. They hadn't bothered to warm up, so nobody was on pitch, and half the instruments didn't produce more than a shrill squeak, but Mr. Thorntonberry didn't seem to care. He continued to pump his hands as every instrument blurted out some wretched noise or another, pointing to various sections of the band, begging for crescendos to music that was already loud enough to wake the dead and horrid enough to kill them all over again.

Bryan stared at the page, unblinking, his fingers working frantically. He wasn't even sure the other two saxophones sitting next to him were playing in the same key, and he was certain they weren't in the same spot. Above Bryan the lights began to flicker, maybe in rhythm to the music, if there actually was one.

"Yes. Fantastic!" Mr. Thorntonberry growled. "Keep it up! Music is the language of the soul!"

If that's the case, there's not a soul alive who would understand what we're saying, Bryan thought. Still, he tried to follow along. The tempo was insane, and Thorntonberry was gesticulating like he was being electrocuted, thrusting his hands this way and that, shaking and trembling and calling out commands like

Moses on the mountain. "Trombones! Now clarinets! Timpani! Bring it up! Louder! Louder!"

Then he pointed to Bryan with his baton.

"Saxophone solo!" he cried.

Bryan pointed to himself, tried to find his place on the page. He was completely lost.

"Stand up!" the music teacher shouted.

"What?"

"Stand up, Bryan! This is your moment. Seize it. SEIZE IT!" Mr. Thorntonberry was beckoning to him with both hands now. Bryan looked over at the drum section, where Myra, frantically working the snare, somehow managed to look at him and shrug.

He stood up and looked back down at his music.

And all of a sudden he could see them, the notes he was supposed to play, falling down along the page. Ds and Gs and As and F-sharps and all the ones in between, marching toward the bottom, much the same as his math problems had this morning. Except this time they were all color-coded. The Cs were blue, the Gs green, and so on. Bryan looked at Mr. Thorntonberry uncertainly, then back down at his dancing music.

Then he brought his sax to his lips and blurted out the note at the bottom of the page.

MISS.

He didn't get it. He'd screwed up the fingering. The word flashed red across the sheet music at the top, and Bryan could actually hear a boo come from somewhere—the trumpet section, maybe? He tried for the next note and then the next, doing better with each. **OKAY**, it told him, and, **GOOD**. Then he hit a string of three in a row.

PERFECT. GREAT. PERFECT.

And suddenly he was on a roll, hitting each note in stride, tapping his foot to the rhythm in his head, blocking out the cacophony of bleating horns and piping winds around him, just concentrating on hitting every color-coded note as it fell off the page. On the podium, Mr. Thorntonberry continued to flail like a hooked fish, stabbing in Bryan's direction with the point of his baton at practically every beat.

And then something miraculous happened. Somehow the rest of the band seemed to fall into place, finding their spots on the page. The drum section got the tempo right, pulling the rhythm together. The trumpets let loose with a fanfare that was completely in sync. One of the clarinets, Tara Spangler, stood up and joined in on Bryan's solo, making it a duet. Mr. Thorntonberry cried out in ecstasy. "Yes! Yes! Bring it! *BA-RING IT!*"

And it actually started to sound . . . *good*. Or at least not horrible. It was like watching a train wreck in reverse, the jackknifed cars suddenly righting themselves on the track, pulling back into line, the smoke and fire from the wreckage disappearing as they recoupled themselves, forming an orderly procession, till everything was back in motion, moving backward, gaining speed. Bryan did an elaborate run of high notes, somehow hitting every single one in succession, holding the last for a full ten seconds as the words **KILLER SOLO** danced across his page. He sucked in a deep breath.

That's when Mr. Thorntonberry tore his sequined vest off, Incredible Hulk style, and threw it in the direction of Weston Roland, the oboe player, who caught it with his flushed-pink face. Bryan's hands trembled. The lights continued to flicker. He didn't even bother to sit down, just blew even louder into his horn. The whole thing crescendoed, a surf of notes cresting, colliding, but for once, in perfect harmony. Mr. Thorntonberry's eyes were wild, his lips trembling. "Yes! Staccato! Percussion! Flutes! Hold it! Hold it! Hooooold it and . . . skabam!"

The bandleader threw his arms up in triumph as the music came to an abrupt halt. He was panting. Everyone was panting. Bryan was exhausted. From somewhere, seemingly from everywhere, he heard the roar of applause, though nobody in the room was actually clapping. Then, just above Thorntonberry's head, Bryan saw the words.

+100 XP.

That's when he realized he was still standing. Just he and Mr. Thorntonberry. The restless bandleader turned and bowed with a flourish of his hands. "We are the music-makers," he said breathlessly, looking right at Bryan. "And we are the dreamers of dreams." Bryan felt a rush as all eyes turned to him, felt himself swell up inside. The applause was real now. Beside him, Mikey let out a piercing whistle.

Then the applause vanished.

Mr. Vincent, the assistant principal, stood at the door, clearing his throat.

"Mr. Biggins," he said, looking toward the saxophone section, where Bryan was still standing. "Principal Petrowski would like a word with you."

From the back of the room Archie Goldman blurted out a *bruh-bruh-brummm* on his tuba.

Nobody laughed.

2:49 P.M.
THE BOSS

THE RECEPTION AREA TO THE PRINCIPAL'S OFFICE
looked inviting enough to the random parent passing through. There were posters plastered all along the walls. Some were student works. Others were pictures of jets in flight or giant sequoias or too-happy tweens reading books, imploring anyone who cared to "achieve," to "grow," and to "learn." The secretary's desk had a jar full of chocolate kisses left over from last Christmas, and the door to Principal Petrowski's office was actually decorated with a rainbow pouring out of a beaming circle of sunshine. It all had the

effect of making Bryan want to throw up. Of course, he'd been feeling that way for most of the day.

Mr. Vincent motioned for Bryan to have a seat facing the rainbow, then whispered something to the secretary before leaving. She turned and gave Bryan a sympathetic smile. Save for the clacking of the secretary's press-on nails against the keyboard, there was hardly any sound in the waiting area. Bryan looked up at the clock. In about an hour he was supposed to meet Wattly behind the school, where, he assumed, Tank would simply roll over him with the treads of his boots, leaving behind the imprint of Bryan's broken body as a memorial for Oz and Myra to lay flowers on. It was a dreadful prospect, but the more Bryan watched the rainbow door, the more he wondered if there were worse things than being clobbered by Chris Wattly.

He had never been to the principal's office before.

The secretary's intercom buzzed to life. "Ms. Mardel—if Mr. Biggins is out there, please send him in." The secretary motioned Bryan toward the office.

Bryan stood up and walked, slowly, like someone trudging through three feet of wet snow, passing through the rainbow door. Principal Petrowski was hunched over his desk, which was messier than Bryan's room at home. He had his head in his hands, dark-brown hair, smooth as an oil slick, brushed backward to cover a peeking crown. He wore a suit, like always; dark gray, like always.

The students had a nickname for Petrowski. They called him the Boss, partly because he was the princi-pal, but mostly because he always wore the same thing to school. Gray suit. White shirt. Black shoes. Even on Show Your Spirit Day, when the other teachers wore sweatshirts with Mount Comfort's golden-maned mas-cot on them. On those days he wore a charcoal suit with a yellow tie.

Today his tie was bloodred, like a gash had opened up down the middle of his chest. On his desk was a coffee mug sporting a quote—"Obedience to the law is demanded as a right; not asked as a favor," which explained one thing, at least—and a letter opener that looked more like a sacrificial dagger. On his walls hung a variety of diplomas and awards. The whole room smelled of coffee and the sweat of tortured kids.

"Please. Have a seat," Petrowski said, motioning to the uncomfortable-looking wooden chairs across from

INSERT COIN TO CONTINUE

him. Bryan sat, trying to scrunch up, making himself as small a target as possible. He was afraid to look in the man's eyes, but even more afraid to look away. Looking away, he knew, was an admission of guilt, and Bryan wasn't sure what, exactly, he was in here for.

It could be so very many things.

The Boss smiled broadly, showcasing a silver-capped tooth, then shuffled through some of the papers on his desk. "You know what I hate most about this job, Biggins?" he asked as he shuffled. "It's all the paper. So much paper. Eight rain forests' worth. Every day I come in and there are at least a hundred pieces of paper sitting on my desk. And most of it is pointless. Absolute junk. Requisitions and policy changes and addendums to some stupid law I've never even heard of. Notes from parents. Notes from the secretary. Flyers for fund-raisers. I just don't have time for it. I hate paper, Biggins. Just despise it. But here I am. Surrounded by it."

Principal Petrowski continued to sort through the slush, finally finding the single sheet of paper that interested him. "Here we go. Bryan Biggins." He grunted. "You, sir, have had a busy day."

Bryan almost laughed. "Busy" was one word for it. He folded his hands in his lap. Unfolded them. Folded them. He didn't say anything. The Boss trailed his finger down a series of handwritten comments, which Bryan strained to read. "Says here you've been wandering the halls without a pass?"

Of course. The Eye of Krug. She'd ratted him out. He should have guessed. She and the Boss even wore matching outfits. He probably let her drink out of the quotable mug. Bryan swallowed and licked his lips. "I ran some errands for teachers today," he squeaked out.

The Boss nodded. "And it also says that you took a snack from the teachers' lounge."

"A Twinkie, sir. Out of the vending machine. I paid for it, though." Bryan shifted from one cheek to the other, trying to get comfortable and failing.

Principal Petrowski set the sheet of paper down on top of the pile. Bryan could see that it was covered in red. His eyes fixated on the Boss's tie. "You understand why we call it the teachers' lounge?"

"Yes, sir."

"It's a lounge. For teachers."

"Yes, sir."

"Teachers'. Lounge."

"Yes, sir." Bryan wondered how many times he had to say "yes, sir."

"And the vending machine *inside* the teachers' lounge. Also for teachers."

"But I—"

"And the snacks *inside* the vending machine. Also for *teachers*." Bryan kept his mouth shut. Petrowski took up the paper again. "So you wandered the halls without permission and took food from the teachers' lounge during third period. Then, during sixth period, you broke one of Mr. McKellen's brooms. Is that correct?"

"That's on there too?" Bryan craned his neck to get a look at the sheet. "I fell on it trying to capture Mr. Mouskerson," he said, then realized just how ridiculous *that* sounded. "I mean, I was on a quest, uh, mission. . . . I was doing something for Mr. Tomlins . . . sir."

"And was that before or after you tackled Amy Krug in the hallway?" the Boss wanted to know.

"Tackled *her*? She tackled *me*!"

Or at least she'd tried to. Bryan guessed they'd ended up kind of tackling each other, if such a thing was possible. He still felt bad for leaving her there on the floor. Though he was feeling a lot less bad about it now that she'd turned him in.

Principal Petrowski was staring at him, tapping one knuckle against his desk.

Bryan lowered his voice. "Sorry, sir. You're right. I shouldn't have been out in the halls without a pass. And I shouldn't have gone into the teachers' lounge. I'm just having a *really* off day."

Principal Petrowski nodded, his normally rigid features softening for a moment. "I can appreciate that," he said. "We all have those days."

"Not like this," Bryan blurted out, then shrank even farther down into his seat. He hadn't meant to say that out loud. But the Boss didn't argue. Instead he turned and looked out the only window in his office, hands folded in his lap.

"Here's what I *should* do," he said, his back still to Bryan. "I *should* call your parents. I *should* write this up and put it in your file. But you know what that would mean, don't you?"

Bryan thought about it for a second. "More paper?" he ventured.

"Precisely. Even more paper. So here's what we are going to do instead. We are going to settle this. Like men." The Boss twisted back around in his chair, and Bryan saw he was making a fist with his right hand.

A fist. Bryan was about to get punched. By the principal. Forget Wattly. Principal Petrowski weighed almost two hundred pounds, and he was about to throw down right in the middle of the office. All those rules about no physical contact and the laws against corporal punishment, yet Bryan was about to have his teeth knocked out by the Boss. He put his hands up in protest. He started to say something about it being illegal to break students' noses, when Principal Petrowski opened his left palm and put his right fist on top of it.

"Rock, paper, scissors," he said.

"What?" Bryan shook his head, confused.

"Rock, paper, scissors. Come on. You kids play it all the time. I've seen you. You win and I let you walk out of here and we forget this whole day ever happened. I win and you call your parents and tell them you are suspended for violating school policy."

Bryan just stared at the principal's fist poised above his other hand. He was serious. He was going to settle this with a game of RPS. As if they were back on the playground in the third grade trying to decide who had to be "it" first. At least, he *looked* serious. Then again, he always looked serious. That's why they called him the Boss.

"Really? I win and I just walk out of here?" Bryan asked. He would have laughed at how ludicrous it all was if it weren't his school record on the line. Though in some ways that just made it even more ridiculous.

"Son," Petrowski said with a sigh. "People like to pretend that life is complicated and full of drama and major decisions and whatnot, but it's really not. It's just one big game. Win or lose, you got no choice—you just keep playing. Now, are we going to do this or should I just hand you the phone and have you call home?"

Bryan opened his left hand and made a fist with his right. "Okay. I'm ready."

He and Principal Petrowski both raised their fists. Then drove them down three times, chanting in unison. "Rock. Paper. Scissors. Shoot."

When he shot, Bryan shut his eyes. He wasn't sure why. Instinct, maybe. Or just afraid to look. He felt his sweaty fist slamming into his even sweatier palm and held it there, fingers closed but his whole arm quivering. He cracked one eye open. Then the other.

Sure enough, Principal Petrowski sat across the desk, making a pair of scissors with his right hand.

"You win," he said, shrugging. "Congratulations." He didn't seem at all unhappy about it. In fact, he seemed to be a little relieved. Bryan saw the flash of blue above the principal's head.

+50 XP.

"You hate paper," Bryan said.

Petrowski nodded. "And you can say you beat the Boss. Except you're not allowed. Can't let anyone know that I let you off the hook. I'd get a reputation for being soft. So you keep this just between you and me, and hopefully we never have to make that phone call to your folks. Understood?"

Bryan nodded. As he did, the final bell rang above them. School was over. He'd made it.

But not really. Not yet.

"It's Friday. The weekend. Go on. Get out of here," the principal said, shooing Bryan out of the chair with a hand that was now shaped like paper. "I really don't want to see your face in my office again."

Bryan stood up and grabbed his backpack, and for a moment he considered telling Petrowski about everything, the whole day, or maybe just the thing about Wattly. After all, if anyone had the power to step in and put an end to it, surely it was the Boss. He could have Wattly called down. Give him a talking to. Maybe call *his* parents. It would stop the fight, at least.

Then again, that might only make it worse.

Bryan opened the door and was met by the poster of the sequoia tree telling him to grow. The Boss called out his name from behind. "And, Biggins . . ."

Bryan turned around, priming himself for the last words of wisdom, the parting shot from the head honcho that would put everything in perspective and would give him some clue as to how to deal with his chaotic, upside-down, and totally insane life.

"Stay out of the teachers' lounge, will ya?" the Boss said.

Then he started restacking his papers.

3:15 P.M.
CROSSING THE LINE

THE HALLS ERUPTED, A HULLABALOO OF FLEEING students, banged lockers, sharp whistles, and barbaric yawps. The foolish teachers stood in their doorways and begged kids not to turn into an unruly mob; the smart ones dashed to their cars to get out before the buses.

As he waded through the steady stream of bodies, Bryan couldn't help but notice the sudden hush that followed him, almost as if he were walking underwater. Every conversation stopped, just for the one second it took to pass him, and then started up again, his mere presence silencing anyone in range. Quietly he made it to his locker, looking desperately for Oz, but the Wizard of Elmhurst Park had vanished.

It didn't make sense. He should have been there. Even though Bryan biked home and Oz took the bus, they always walked out together. Bryan stood by his locker, pretending to be invisible, scanning the hall, looking for a friendly face. It didn't have to be Oz, really. Myra, Rajesh, Juan—anyone would be fine, just so long as he wasn't alone. He waited as long as he dared—two, three minutes—then grabbed his phone and sent Oz a text.

Where R U?

Bryan waited fifteen seconds. No reply.

Maybe he was already outside. He knew Bryan had gone to see the Boss. Everyone in band had watched Bryan walk the concrete mile. Maybe Oz was counting on him being late. Bryan shouldered his backpack and merged with the herd, keeping his nose to the ground, headed for the door. No sign of Oz. No sign of Wattly, either, though.

He stepped outside and looked up. The rain had stopped, finally, the clouds shifting from gunmetal

INSERT COIN TO CONTINUE

gray to sun-brightened platinum. Everything was still soaked through—lake-size puddles saddled the curbs, and students had to be careful to avoid the waterfalls from the broken gutters. The whole world felt heavy, sagging, ready to collapse. *Let it*, Bryan thought. *I've saved it once already.*

Oz rode bus 22, which looked almost full, though Bryan didn't see his best friend's profile in the windows. He checked his phone again. Still no messages. Where did that boy run off to? The engines purred. The first bus in the line was already starting to pull away. Bryan took one last look around.

He felt a tap on his shoulder. He hoped it was Oz. He feared it was Wattly. He was afraid to find out.

"Long day?"

Bryan felt a shudder of relief followed immediately by a whole new wave of nervousness. It was Jess. She stood right next to him, close enough that he instinctively took a step back, her hands on the straps of her pack, bottom lip tucked under her top teeth. Her mud-puddle eyes held him steady.

Bryan shoved his hands into his pockets, as if he were afraid of what they might do if left to roam free.

In the past it had sometimes taken him a full minute to summon the courage and composure just to say "hi" to Jess, but this afternoon the words seemed to come a little easier.

"So you heard about my day?" he asked.

He hoped she hadn't heard *everything*. He had done quite a few things today that he wasn't exactly proud of. And maybe a few that he was. Hiding in the girls' bathroom wasn't a high point, for example, and was just the kind of thing he hoped hadn't been picked up on Jess's radar.

"I heard you tackled Amy Krug," she said.

That was probably another low point. Bryan itched with embarrassment, freeing one hand long enough to scratch the back of his neck. He could tell Jess was trying hard not to laugh. He sort of wished she would stop trying. It would be worth hearing the sound of her laughter, even if it was at his expense. "Tackled is such a strong word. I kind of just fell on top of her."

Bryan frowned, regretting how that sounded, but Jess was still grinning.

"Well, is it true, at least, that you wrestled a giant rat in the janitors' closet?"

Mr. Mouskerson hardly counted as a giant rat, and flinging the little beast out of his pant leg hardly counted as wrestling, but it was nice to hear his legend spreading.

"It was the boiler room, actually. And it was just a mouse," Bryan said. He noticed the look of mock disappointment on Jess's face. "But it did try to attack me. A cunning and vicious creature." Nearly all the buses had pulled away now. Still no sign of Oz. It didn't matter quite so much anymore, though. "How about you?" he finally managed to ask. "How was your day?"

"Over," she said. "You're not supposed to be on one of those buses, are you?"

"I usually bike home." Already this conversation was longer than any they had had in the last three years. "I thought you walked?"

"I do." Jess nodded. "Just not by myself. Not that I can't. I just prefer to have company."

"Right," Bryan said. Company. Blond, perfect, shiny company. With great teeth. She was probably just standing here waiting for Prince to arrive. Except she wasn't looking around. She was looking at Bryan.

Not just looking. She actually nudged him with her eyebrows. At least, he thought it was a nudge, a little hint, a fill-in-the-blank kind of gesture. Distinctly pointed at him.

"You mean?"

Jess shrugged. "It's not that far," she said, as if that mattered.

Bryan felt a tingle work its way to the tips of his ears. He looked behind him. He could see the baseball diamond and the teachers' parking lot, and the little alley behind the old playground. The one with the Dumpsters where you could conveniently hide the body of a dead middle schooler. He turned back to Jess, who was watching him, eyebrows still arched, waiting for an answer. He could almost hear the timer ticking down in his head. Oz might be looking for him. Wattly was probably tearing the heads off of stray kittens and drinking their blood as some kind of prefight ritual. And the girl he'd been crushing on for four years was staring at him for a change. Why, he couldn't be sure, but he wasn't going to question it.

"Yeah. Okay," he said.

Jess smiled and brushed by him. The last bus pulled out into the street. "Let's go, then," she said.

They walked across the school's front lawn, through

INSERT COIN TO CONTINUE

the damp grass, past the bronze statue of the Mount Comfort lion, captured in midleap. Jess walked beside him, not touching but close enough that he could grab her hand if he dared. Yet even having faced the likes of Reynolds, Wang, and Baylor-Tore hadn't given him *that* much nerve. Instead Bryan tried to be cool, afraid that if he smiled, his face might break in half. He hadn't walked next to her since the fourth grade when they were line leaders.

"I heard you got called down to the Boss's office," she said, a hint of admiration in her voice.

"That was only twenty minutes ago!" Bryan sputtered.

"Yeah. Jamie C., who plays flute, texted Kasarah, who texted me. You know how this place is. If it's nobody's business, you can be sure everybody knows about it. Was it terrible? Were there handcuffs on the chairs? I heard he straps you in and shines a bright lamp in your face."

"It wasn't that bad," Bryan said. "He just gave me a lecture. But if you should ever find yourself paying Petrowski a visit, just remember to always choose rock."

"What?"

JOHN DAVID ANDERSON

Bryan shook his head. "Sorry. Forget it. You'll probably never be called down to the principal's office anyway."

Jess smirked. "Don't be so sure," she said.

They pulled up at the street and stood on the curb. Mount Comfort Road was bustling, much busier than usual, and nobody seemed to care that it was a school zone either. Most of the cars had to be going at least fifty in a twenty zone. If there had been a cop there, he could have pulled over an entire parade full of cars.

"I've never seen it this busy," Jess remarked as a pickup truck zoomed past, spraying water that just missed their feet. Bryan nodded. The street was packed both ways. Six lanes full. Unusual, to say the least.

At least, it would be unusual on any other day.

"We should probably just walk down to the light and cross there," Jess suggested, pointing to the school entrance a ways down.

Suddenly Bryan saw a path open before him. He knew what he had to do. "Nah," he said. "We can make it." He looked left, then right. Then he took a deep breath and counted to three before doing the very thing he'd told himself he couldn't only minutes ago. He grabbed Jess's hand.

INSERT COIN TO CONTINUE

"Trust me," he said.

And then he pulled her out into the busy road.

He could hear her screaming behind him, but Jess's voice was drowned out by the beeping of the car that zipped past in the next lane over. He felt her grip tighten, trying to break his fingers, as they sprinted across the first two lanes of traffic before Bryan pulled them both to an abrupt stop to let a truck zoom in front of them, so close Bryan could have reached over and tweaked the passenger's nose through his open window. Another pickup barreled toward them in the middle lane, its driver laying on his horn. Bryan dodged right, took three steps, and then leaped for the median, pulling Jess alongside. She crashed into him, nearly knocking him off the curb into the oncoming traffic headed the other way.

"Are you *crazy*?" she shouted, nearly breathless, her fingers clenched, knuckle-white, in his.

"I think so. Yeah," he said, his eyes on the traffic, watching the pattern, waiting for the right moment. It was a matter of reflexes. He could feel his muscles twitch. Cars and trucks shot by on either side. The median was only two feet wide and his Breeches of Enduring Stiffness were buffeted by spray from puddles. He squeezed Jess's hand. "Ready?" he asked.

"No!" she shouted.

Bryan bolted off the median anyway, dragging her into the street with another shriek. A car darted in front of them. Another behind. A third actually swerved around them, its driver calling out a few names that Bryan had never been called before. He heard the long bellow of a semi's horn passing in front of them and turned to see another car closing fast. He held his breath, waiting for the truck to pass, and then tugged hard on Jess's hand, pulling both of them across the final lane and into the grass beyond.

The grass was slicker than the pavement. Bryan's feet slid beneath him and he dropped, pulling Jess with him, the two of them tumbling down the slope of the drainage ditch, soaking their backs on the wet grass and coming to a rest only a foot from the sloppy mud bottom.

Bryan felt Jess wrench her hand free. He was afraid to look at her. She was mad. That had been stupid. And dangerous. He wasn't sure what had come over him. He'd seen an opening and he'd taken it.

Jess sat up. She turned to face him. "That was—"

"Idiotic," he said, saving her the trouble.

"*Completely* idiotic," she repeated, then her voice softened. "And kind of fun." She shook her head and smiled up at the sky. Bryan looked back at the convoy of cars skimming through the puddles on Mount Comfort Road. Already, it seemed, the traffic was starting to thin out and slow down.

"You wanna go again?"

Jess looked down at the slick grass. "I think I'm dirty enough already." She stood up and twisted around. Sure enough, the back of her jeans was streaked with mud. She shrugged, then bent over and offered her hand. Bryan took it and let her pull him up. She craned her neck to look behind him.

"Yours isn't so bad," she said. Then with one hand she brushed the back of his jeans. He felt his face get hot and hoped she wouldn't notice, just as he barely noticed the blue letters now floating in the air above them.

+50 XP.

For what, exactly, he wasn't sure. For being brave or stupid or both. For jumping across six lanes of traffic. For making it to the other side.

"Did you see that?" he asked.

"See what?"

Bryan shook his head. "Nothing. Don't worry about it." He wasn't sure why he'd even asked. He just thought/hoped that maybe Jess, of all people, could tell him he wasn't crazy.

Instead she told him to come on, and to try not to get her killed again.

They passed a gas station and a church and turned into a neighborhood full of older houses, nicer than Bryan's but only a little. As they walked, he asked her how her day had *really* gone. She already knew enough about his. The whole school knew. And yet, strangely, they really had no idea. She started telling him how she had been selected to be a photographer for the yearbook.

"It's called 'Reflections in Time.' How awful is that?"

Bryan admitted it was pretty bad. He didn't think he was going to bother getting a yearbook. He could think of only about seven people who would sign it, and three of them were teachers. Though if Jess was taking pictures for it, he supposed he would have to. She pointed down a road to her right.

"If you turn down that way and go, like, six blocks,

you hit our elementary school. Do you remember Ms. Buttes?"

"Of course," Bryan said. Ms. Buttes was their third-grade teacher. The year he and Jess first met. He remembered very little about the woman except that no one ever pronounced her name right. On purpose. It was supposed to be pronounced "Boo-tez." But they were third graders, so it was always Butts.

"Yeah, so my mom and I ran into her at the grocery store the other day and found out she got married to Mr. Mackin, the music teacher."

"I remember Mr. Mackin," Bryan said. He had no hair and two chins.

"Right. Apparently they are just made for each other, but when they got married, she hyphenated the last name, so now . . ."

She stopped walking and waited for it to sink in, staring at him expectantly. It took a moment, but then Bryan snorted laughter. "Mrs. Buttsmackin'? Oh my God, that's so sweet."

"I know, right?" She laughed right alongside him. It was kind of musical. Even better than band practice. *Much* better than band practice.

"Third grade was awesome."

"It was, wasn't it?" She reached up with one hand and retucked that same loose sprig of hair behind her ear. Bryan started to think she shook it loose just so she could put it back whenever he was around.

All down the block the backyards were filling up with younger kids—some of them probably third graders—finishing their after-school snacks and playing make-believe games, completely oblivious, Bryan thought, to what they were in for in a few years. "Speaking of third grade," he said hesitantly, "you remember how everybody always brought treats for, like, everything? Little goody bags with cheap pencils and stale candy for, like, birthdays and Halloween and stuff."

"Earth Day. Kiss Your Grandmother Day. Teacher Appreciation Day," she answered.

"And you had to bring a bag for everyone, even the kids you didn't like," Bryan mused.

"I liked everybody," Jess said, smiling.

"You lie."

Jess shook her head. "I'm serious. I liked everybody. It's not until you grow up that you realize what jerks some people are."

Bryan hoped she didn't mean him. He had a whole list of people he thought were jerks. That list hadn't gotten any shorter today. "You couldn't have liked everybody. Nobody likes *everybody*."

"In third grade I did. In our class I did."

"Even Robbie Vaughn?"

Robbie Vaughn was the really weird kid in third grade. Like, fifty times weirder than Oz, which made him at least a hundred times weirder than Bryan. Bryan once caught Robbie licking the sidewalk, that's how strange he was. His family moved away two years ago. Probably a good thing, or else he would have ended up going to middle school with Tank Wattly. Then Robbie's parents would be scraping him off the school parking lot too.

"Robbie Bug-Kisser? He was sweet," Jess said. "He had really big eyes, though." Bryan made his own eyes bug out of his head. He could tell she didn't want to laugh. "He was a *little* odd, I guess."

Bryan took a deep breath. "And do you remember Valentine's Day? I don't know, you must have forgotten to hand all of yours out or something because after class you came up to me and gave me an envelope.

And it had one of those candy hearts in it. The ones that taste like chalk. Do you remember?"

He wasn't looking at her. He couldn't look at her. They were both looking at the road unfolding before them, the mail truck parked alongside, the dogs barking, balking at invisible fences. He noticed her shake her head out of the corner of his eye, though.

"You know, the little pastel ones?" he pressed. "With the messages? And the one you gave me was white with red letters that you could barely read."

BE MINE, it said, but Bryan couldn't bring himself to say that part.

Jess shook her head again. "What did it say? Do you even remember the message?"

Bryan shrugged. "Something stupid, probably," he said. "I was just curious." He stomped at the edge of a puddle, making a small tremor that carried to the other side, distorting his reflection.

"I do remember this one time, though," Jess said, "in the fifth grade. At lunch. With the sandwich?" She looked at him questioningly. Bryan shook his head. "Really? You don't remember? My mother had mixed up my lunch with my dad's, and I got a bologna and mustard sandwich and a note telling me to have a good day at work?"

Bryan tried to think back. He might have a vague recollection of something like that.

"And you must have heard me talking to my friends, even from two tables away, because you came over and asked me if I wanted your peanut butter and jelly with the crusts cut off."

Bryan turned and looked at her finally. She was grinning at the thought of it. Crusts cut off. Yes. He remembered now. It didn't seem like a big deal at the time. Not like giving someone a chalky piece of candy on Valentine's Day.

"You said that bologna was your favorite," Jess continued. "But I watched you. You didn't take a single bite of that sandwich. You just put it back in your lunch box untouched. And I realized you hated it just as much as I did."

She was right. He'd put it back in his box, and when he got home, he'd thrown it away, burying it beneath a used coffee filter so his mom wouldn't ask any questions.

"Just mustard," he said.

"What?"

"I don't mind bologna. It's the mustard I can't stand."

"Me neither," Jess said. She took a deep breath before adding, "It was one of the sweetest things anyone's ever done for me."

Bryan nearly turned into a puddle himself. Had she actually just called him sweet? She hadn't *exactly*, but it was close enough. "I'm sure people do nice things for you all the time," he said. "I'm sure Landon Prince . . ."

Input error. System failure.

He stopped himself from at least finishing the thought, but it was too late. Jess's smile disappeared. She seemed to tense up at hearing Landon's name. If it was possible to kick your own butt without falling over, Bryan would have tried. He looked to the sky for messages in blue writing, options he could choose from, but nothing appeared. He was all on his own with his big mouth.

"Sorry," he said quickly, hoping she would just let it pass and they could keep talking about third grade and bologna sandwiches and the fact that she liked everybody. But the damage was done.

"No. You're right," Jess said, staring now at her

mud-stained shoes. "He's great. I mean, he's Landon Prince, right?" she said with a sigh. "What's not to like? He's cute. And athletic. And popular. He even has good taste in clothes."

Bryan looked down at his Tunic of Unwashing, now with bonus sweat and a spot of Oz's blood on the sleeve. Or maybe that was ketchup. Could be ketchup.

"He gets straight As and he never gets in trouble," Jess continued.

Bryan got As occasionally. And up until today he'd never wrestled with a teacher, tackled a hall monitor, or been sent to the principal's office.

"Plus he's nice to just about everyone, and he helps out at the community center, and his family rescues stray dogs. I mean, he's practically perfect. I'm sure every girl at Mount Comfort thinks so."

They did. At least according to the messages on the girls' bathroom walls, they did, but Bryan figured he shouldn't say that. Instead he thought about the third grade, and Ms. Buttes, and the time when a girl in pigtails handed him an envelope with a candy heart inside. Really? Rescues stray dogs? Suddenly, saving Mr. Mouskerson didn't seem like a big deal.

"I mean, you'd have to be crazy not to like a guy like that," Jess added. She looked at Bryan.

He wanted to ask her if she was crazy. He wanted to ask her so many things, in fact. Did she like *Star Wars*? And did she prefer barbecue chips or sour cream and onion? Dogs or cats? Marvel or DC? What television shows did she watch? Did she know how it made him nuts when she did that hair-tuck thing? He wanted to ask if she ever thought about him, and *what* she thought about him. And why she had invited him to Missy's party. And did she ever write him long e-mails and then delete them because they sounded stupid and cheesy and she was afraid he would just laugh at them and tell all his friends? And did she know that walking down the street with her had made this whole whacked-out day of his almost worth it?

But he couldn't bring himself to say any of those things. He couldn't even bring himself to look her in the eyes. All he could say was, "I guess so."

Jess nodded, then took her phone from her pocket, checked it, and put it back. "My house is that one," she said, pointing down a cul-de-sac to a two-story colonial trimmed in brown to match her eyes. "Thanks for walking me."

Bryan still didn't look up from the puddle-splotched street. "No problem," he murmured.

"Okay. Well. See you around." Jess turned to go, made it about ten steps, then stopped and turned back. "It's after four, by the way," she said from across the street. "Just thought you should know." Then she turned and disappeared into her house.

After four. Why would she . . .

Bryan shook his head, then fished in his backpack for his own phone, double-checking the time. It was ten after four.

Four o'clock. The Dumpsters behind the diamond. He had missed it. Walking home with Jess, he had lost all track of time. He had lost all track of everything.

Suddenly it dawned on him. That's why she'd done it. She knew. Of course she knew. Everybody knew.

Bryan looked toward her house, but she was already inside, the door shut behind her. She had made his decision for him, distracted him on purpose. Made certain he was somewhere else when his time to meet Wattly rolled around.

JOHN DAVID ANDERSON

Which meant . . . it meant . . . Bryan wasn't sure, but he knew it meant something. Maybe it meant he should go knock on her door. Tell her that he remembered exactly what the message on the valentine candy heart was. Tell her about the lip gloss that he'd saved. Okay, maybe not that. That was a little too weird. But he would at least tell her that it was okay to be crazy.

Maybe tell her he was crazy too.

Bryan's phone buzzed, startling him.

It was a text message. From Oz. But not really from Oz.

U R late, it said. *I am still waiting.*

And I have your friend.

4:37 P.M.
MIDDLE SCHOOL KOMBAT

BRYAN HAD TO STOP LONG ENOUGH TO CATCH HIS breath. He wasn't used to running that far. He looked across the parking lot at the face of Mount Comfort Middle School. There were pockets of students waiting for their rides from chess club or cheer practice. A procession of parents honking their horns and waving impatiently. The drum corps for the school's marching band was just now filing out through the double doors. But no sign of Oz anywhere. Or his captors.

Bryan hadn't shown up when he was supposed to. A big enough deal. But now he realized it was more complicated than that. Now it was a hostage situation.

He had forgotten to take his phone off vibrate after school, so he'd missed the previous twelve messages and the one panicked phone call. All he got was the text message from Wattly saying that if he didn't show, then Oz would pay the price. Bryan glanced over at the bike rack and thought about making a run for it; let Oz fend for himself. He was the one who'd gotten Bryan into this mess to begin with.

But he knew there was no way he could do that to his friend. Wattly was going to get his hands on Bryan one way or another. This was what the whole day had been building to, after all. All roads led here. Tennenbaum. The mouse. The Boss. Even Jess. All side quests. There was only one way this day was ever going to end.

Bryan walked cautiously through the parking lot and around the back of the school. He didn't even make it to the alley and its Dumpsters. They spotted him from across the baseball diamond and immediately came to intercept.

There were only four of them. Three of Wattly's football buddies—Zach Rollins and Bobby Mizaro and some kid Bryan and Oz just called Mr. Happy Face because he always looked supremely ticked off. And Tank, of course, rolling steadily toward him. Squished between the four of them was Oz. Bryan had expected a ringside audience complete with bookies and commentators ready to dish out a play-by-play. *Wattly delivers a punch, and there go all of Biggins's teeth, straight down his throat.* Maybe there had been. Maybe the crowd had waited for a while and then given up. He pictured Mikey Gerard throwing his two dollars on the ground in disgust. It was a small consolation, knowing that nobody else would see him get pulverized.

Except Oz. But that was okay. He wanted Oz to watch. When his spine was crushed and he was confined to a wheelchair, Bryan decided, Oz was going to be solely responsible for pushing him around and feeding him applesauce.

Their eyes met and Oz put a hand up in a pathetic wave. He had some grass stains on his knee, and the swollen nose from gym, but that was a basketball's work. No bruises or scrapes. They stopped with twenty feet between them. Tank looked even bigger than usual, casting his shadow so far in front of him that it nearly stretched to Bryan's feet. Bryan noticed Wattly had one hand on Oz's shoulder and was squeezing hard enough to give Oz a hunch.

"You finally decided to show up," Tank said.

Greetings, chosen one. I have been expecting you.

He looked at least six feet tall. Sure, he'd had to repeat a grade, but no thirteen-year-old should be that tall. Bryan nodded toward Oz. "Let 'im go, Chris," Bryan said. "He has nothing to do with this." It seemed like the right thing to say, even if it wasn't at all true, even if Oz was just as much to blame—if not entirely.

The Wizard of Elmhurst Park began to blubber. "Bryan, I am *so* sorry. I was ambushed, I swear. They snuck up behind me. There was nothing I could—"

Oz didn't finish his thought because Tank gave him a one-handed shove that sent him stumbling into the waiting arms of Rollins, then motioned toward the empty bleachers behind the dugouts. Wattly's three friends dragged Oz through the mud. He had stopped talking, but the look in his eyes screamed one word.

Run.

Maybe four words, once you added *for your life.*

Bryan shook his head. He couldn't just leave Oz with Wattly and his goons. He carefully considered his other options. He was pretty sure Tank couldn't spell the word "diplomacy," let alone know what it stood for, but it was worth a try.

"Listen, Tank. I'm sorry for what I said. I shouldn't have said it. I probably shouldn't have even thought it. And I promise you, I never said anything about your mother being stupid. Somebody made that up."

Tank shrugged. "To be honest, I could care less what you say about her. We don't really get along. But you can't go around bad-mouthing me to people, hobbit, and just get away with it. I have a rep to consider." Wattly advanced as he spoke, only ten feet away now. On the bleachers Oz was surrounded. He had his hands clasped over his eyes, afraid to watch.

"I'm not going to fight you, Chris," Bryan said. He had heard somewhere, in a movie maybe, that if you used peoples' first names, it humanized them. Made them like you more or something.

It didn't work.

"I don't expect it to be a fight, really," Wattly said. "That's why I'm going to do you a favor and at least give you the first shot before I break your nose." Tank took another step closer.

Then let us begin, warrior, so I can wallow in a bath of your cruor.

Bryan didn't want anyone bathing in his cruor. He wanted to keep his cruor inside his body where it belonged. He took a step back, keeping the buffer between them. "Seriously, man, what is this going to prove? That you're stronger than me? I don't think that was ever in question. I'm just a waste of your time." All else fails, defer to the enemy's sense of superiority. Give him enough lip service and maybe he won't bust your own lips open.

That didn't work either, though.

"Are you kidding? I've been looking forward to this all day." Tank reached out with one hand and gave Bryan a shove. "What are you waiting for?"

"I'm not going to hit you," Bryan said.

Another push. Hand to the face this time. Wattly's hand smelled like boiled ham. Bryan stumbled two steps back.

"Come on, Biggins. Do it already. Right here." Wattly pointed to his chin. "Who knows? Maybe you'll take me out in one shot. Maybe today is your lucky day."

Wattly thrust his face into Bryan's. Bryan stared at that chin, with its fissure and its swath of fuzz, punctuating a face that he had dreaded seeing from the moment he stepped foot in the halls of Mount Comfort Middle School. How many times had he daydreamed about doing just what Chris was asking him to? Or fantasized about Wattly choking on a green bean at school and keeling over? Maybe today *was* his lucky day. Bryan felt his toes curl, followed by his fingers. Wattly reached out with both hands.

This time Bryan was shoved hard enough to tumble onto the wet dirt of the pitcher's mound. His bag fell from his shoulder as he landed on his already-bruised backside.

Wattly sneered down at him. Bryan heard a bass drum start to thud from the opposite side of the school. Starting low and slow at first. *Thwump. Thwump. Thwump. Thwump.*

"Stand up."

"No."

"Come on, Biggins!"

"No," Bryan spit. Every part of him felt brittle, stretched so thin he felt he might tear in half in the wind. His bottom lip quivered. The pounding of the drums grew faster. Louder. *Thwump, thwump, thwump.*

"Stand up, coward!"

Wattly's face was half obscured in the sunlight slinking behind him. He didn't look evil. Just determined. His eyes didn't burn with rage the way the Demon King's did in Sovereign of Darkness. They just looked kind of empty, like two black marbles. But Tank's mouth was set in a sneer, a grin that told Bryan how much he was enjoying this. Standing over him. Taunting him.

Daring him.

Bryan pulled himself back to his feet and clenched his teeth.

"There you go, hobbit. That's the spirit!"

From out of nowhere the snare drums joined in with a roll, softly, barely audible over the sound of Bryan's own heartbeat, which continued to thud in time to the deeper drums. Bryan could feel it building, all of it, tightening into a core that started in his chest and pulsed out along his arm to his clenched fingers. When he spoke again, it wasn't much more than a whisper, but he said it slow so even Wattly could understand.

"Promise me that no matter what happens, this will be the end of it."

"What?" Tank said.

"No more threats. No more pushing. No more pranks. We just leave each other alone for the rest of the year. Oz, too."

"Man, when I'm finished, there won't be enough left of you to scrape off of my *shoe*."

"Just promise me," Bryan said.

"Fine. Whatever. But you should know that if this is the last time I ever get to mess with you, I'm going to make the most of it."

The drums paused. Just for a moment. Tank turned and smiled at his friends on the bleachers, looking away, just for a second.

So am I, Bryan thought. And he took his shot.

He swung with everything, and he connected. Fist planted on that big, square jaw. Bryan heard a sickening sound, bone driven into bone through too-thin layers of skin and muscle. Saw Tank's head jerk back and to the side. Felt the driving pain shoot through his own fingers and clear up his arm.

From the other side of the school, the drum corps exploded with sound.

Tank rocked backward, both hands reaching for his jaw with a grunt. Bryan stepped back, shaking out his mashed fingers, bringing his knuckles to his mouth. He saw the words appear in red above Wattly's head, and he felt all the blood rush to his own.

+5 DAMAGE.

He did it. He actually *hit* Tank Wattly. Bryan looked toward the bleachers, saw the stunned looks on all four faces, including Oz, who had taken his hands down and just stared at Bryan with his jaw in his lap. Then Oz pointed, but too late. Bryan saw Wattly's fist just as it drove its way into his gut like a piston firing.

-10 HP.

Bryan doubled over, trying to catch his breath as Wattly advanced, one hand still rubbing his jaw but the other ready to deliver another blow. Bryan dropped to one knee on the pitcher's mound, choking.

"Stand up, Biggins. We're just getting started," Tank growled.

Bryan huddled tight, crouched low but still on his toes. He bit down on his lower lip. It hurt to breathe. He felt Wattly's hand on his jacket, grabbing a fistful, ready to wrench him back onto his feet. Then he grunted and lunged, driving his head between Wattly's legs, wrapping one arm around each of them, sweeping Tank's giant tree trunks out from under him. Wattly hit the ground hard, slamming his head against the packed dirt as Bryan scrambled to his feet. From the bleachers he heard Oz cheer. In the space above Tank's head he saw the letters.

+8 DAMAGE.

Tank got to his feet and spit out a glob of pink saliva, rubbing the back of his head with one hand. From the bleachers Bryan heard someone—Mr. Happy Face?—yell out, "Come on, Tank. Finish this twerp. Coach is going to be ticked enough as it is."

But Wattly didn't look like he'd heard. His eyes were fixed on Bryan. He smiled big enough that Bryan could see the blood in his teeth.

Then he charged.

Bryan stood up straight, then at the last second he rolled to his right. Wattly's hand grabbed again

JOHN DAVID ANDERSON

at Bryan's jacket, nearly tearing it in half, but Bryan pulled himself free, leaving Tank with his back turned. Bryan kicked as hard as he could, driving his foot into the soft spot behind Tank's left knee. Wattly buckled, then took another kick in the side.

COMBO +2.

Wattly turned and lashed out with one hand, but Bryan jumped back in time, then stepped forward with another kick, this one somehow finding Tank's armpit.

COMBO +3.

And lodging there. His foot actually *stuck* in Wattly's armpit, leaving Bryan one-legged, like a floundering flamingo. He struck out with both fists, one to each of Tank's ears. Then twisted his leg free, pulling hard and landing on his back. Above Tank's head he saw:

MAX COMBO. +20 DAMAGE.

Bryan turned and scrambled up to his hands and knees, crawling, when he felt a giant hand grab him by his jeans, pulling him backward. Before he knew it, he was airborne. Literally lifted off the ground by his pants, his underwear riding up painfully. Bryan heard a grunt and then felt weightless for a moment before slamming hard into the ground.

INSERT COIN TO CONTINUE

His teeth jarred against one another. He blinked through black and yellow splotches. He couldn't see above him; there were words there, no doubt, telling him how many hit points he'd just lost—a thousand, probably, that's what it felt like—but he could barely see straight. He flipped over just as Tank's tread buried itself in his side, right beneath his ribs, a swift kick that exploded throughout his whole body. There was a flash of red. Then another and another. Bryan rolled, trying to get away. He felt hands on him, underneath him, pulling him up, wrapping around him, around his neck.

Bryan couldn't breathe. He clawed for Tank's arms. Kicked out with his heels against Tank's shins. He felt dizzy. He was sure he was just going to pass out. In the bleachers everybody was screaming.

Then he remembered something he had seen before. Not in a video game but on TV. About how a 90-pound stick figure of a woman had thwarted a 220-pound burglar who had come up behind her with a knife. Something about leverage and balance. Grabbing in just the right place and twisting just the right way. Pure physics.

JOHN DAVID ANDERSON

Bryan planted his feet, grabbed hold of Wattly's right arm with both hands, and twisted. With a surprised grunt Tank rolled across Bryan's shoulder, all sixty tons of him, headed for the wet grass. But one hand still had hold of Bryan, dragging him down on top of him, both of them crashing to the ground.

Bryan felt himself land hard. Knees first.

He heard a sound. The crash of a cymbal, ringing in the sky.

NOOOOOOOOOOOOOOOO!!!

All the air escaped Wattly's lungs in a cough that turned into a throaty groan. Bryan saw the boy's face instantly purple as he twisted away, hands reaching between his legs, whole body deflating like a burst balloon, curling like a worm stuck on the summer sidewalk.

The letters above Tank's head flashed.

CRITICAL HIT. +50 DAMAGE.

Wattly lay in the grass, whimpering, eyes shut, as Bryan pulled himself woozily to his feet and wavered above. The boy's hands were still cupped between his legs, his body curled up fetal, his face contorted in pain.

"Finish him!"

Bryan turned to see Oz shouting at him from the bleachers.

"FINISH HIM!"

Bryan looked down at Chris's scrunched face, his body a twisted knot, rocking back and forth. One more kick to the face would do it. Break the kid's nose or maybe even knock out his front teeth. He thought about all those times pressed up against the locker. Pushed up against the wall. Books scattered across the floor. All those times he had been told to go back to the Shire. And all the things unheard, whispered by Wattly or someone like him into the ear of some girl, and the laughter that followed. All the writing on the bathroom walls.

He thought about the demon. About how far you had to go to win the game.

Beneath him, Chris Wattly started coughing.

This wasn't a game. He was just a kid. They were both just kids.

Bryan dragged himself slowly back to the pitcher's mound and bent down for his backpack and his jacket, then came back to Tank. He reached into his pocket for his quarter—Oz's quarter—and dropped it on the ground beside Wattly's head.

"Here. You probably need this more than me."

Behind the dugout the rest of Wattly's crew stood up in unison, and for a moment Bryan thought they were going to gang-tackle him. Drag both him and Oz back to the Dumpster and make them eat trash, or just throw them inside and sit on the lid. Bryan walked toward them anyway, knuckles scraped, knees wobbling, bruised and bloodied, but determined not to flinch. They parted wordlessly.

Oz grabbed his bag and galloped down the bleachers, nearly falling over himself. "Dude, that was so . . . ," he started to say, but Bryan cut him off with a cold stare.

"Just shut up and walk," he said.

They started slowly, walking backward. Then a little faster, finally spinning around and daring to breathe. As they crossed the field, Bryan looked back to see Wattly's friends standing over him. They weren't bothering to help him up. They were just staring at him as if he were some strange bug they had discovered and were thinking about stepping on.

And above Chris's body floated familiar words, but Bryan could barely stand to look. It made him sick, seeing them there, Wattly unmoving beneath them.

When he was sure they were far enough away, Bryan stopped and leaned against a tree that had just started shedding. His legs gave out beneath him and he collapsed into the leaves.

Oz took that as his cue to start talking again. "Oh my God, man! Did you *see* that? Did you just see what you just *did*?"

What he just did. Bryan wasn't even sure what he had done. It all blurred in his head. He could still *feel* it, though. Everywhere. From ears to ankles. Everything pulsed and pounded and throbbed.

"You, like, totally obliterated him. He was, like, all, *Grrrrr*, and you were like, *Umm*, and he was like, *Ungh*, and you were like, *Oh yeah? Then take this*, and he was like *slam*, and then you went *crack* and he was all, *Oooohhh*."

Oz grabbed himself and pretended to crumple over, providing a reenactment of the final move. The Tank buster. Knee meets groin. Critical hit. Bryan propped himself up against the tree and rubbed his sore, raw knuckles and inspected the blood on his shirt. Some of it was his now. Some of it was Wattly's. Some of it, still probably Oz's. While Oz danced around, throwing imaginary punches, Bryan took stock of his injuries. From the outside it wasn't that bad. A split lip. No doubt a few bruises. But he felt worse inside. His intestines felt like mashed potatoes.

"I mean, right in the rocks. Direct hit."

"Yeah," Bryan said. He felt under his ribs where Wattly had planted all his toes. It felt like something was already growing there. "How did they get a hold of you, anyway?"

Oz looked down at his feet. "I was looking for you after school," he said. "They figured you wouldn't show, so they found me. Said I was the bait. Where were *you*? I texted you a hundred times!"

Bryan thought about telling him. About Jess. About how they had dodged cars together. About the mustard and the valentine and his own big mouth and all the rest, but it was too hard to explain. His lower lip was swollen. His throat hurt. Besides, Oz was barely even listening. He was still pretend fighting, acting the whole thing out all over again. Bryan pressed gingerly along his forehead, where a lump was already forming.

Suddenly Oz stopped dancing. He looked at Bryan, eyes wide. "Wait. Was that . . . was that *it*?"

"It?" Bryan repeated, but he knew exactly what Oz meant. He pictured the words floating above Wattly's folded body.

+200 XP, the words had said. **LEVEL UP**. Nothing else. But Bryan had faced the Demon King. Vanquished him with a well-placed knee. It was over. Had to be. "Yeah," Bryan said. "That was it."

Oz looked like he was going to pee his pants. He was actually vibrating. "I *knew* it. You totally creamed him. Game over, man. Game. Over."

"Game over," Bryan repeated. He peeled himself off the tree. He felt like he could at least stand now. Maybe even walk, though the houses around him continued to spin. He turned and stumbled down the sidewalk.

"Hey. Wait up. Where are you going?" Oz said, scrambling up next to him.

"Home," Bryan said. "I'm going home. Like you said, it's over."

"Sure. All right. Hang on. I'll just call my mom. Have her come and pick us up."

"No. That's all right. I'm just going to walk, I think," Bryan said, taking a few dizzy steps and then finding his balance.

"But what about your bike?"

"I'll get it later," Bryan mumbled.

"Oh. Okay." Oz stepped into line right behind him. Bryan stopped and turned. He stared at his best friend.

"*I'm* going home, Oz. Just me. You can call your mom and have her come get you."

Oz frowned, eyes scrunched. It took a moment. Finally he nodded. "Oh. All right. Yeah."

"I'll call you tonight," Bryan promised.

"Right. Okay. Whatever you say."

He looked hurt, but Bryan couldn't explain. He just needed to be by himself. He waved good-bye and turned back toward home, just leaving Oz standing there on the sidewalk, sad and alone and confused. Bryan didn't look back. The fight with Wattly had taken everything out of him and left him with . . . what exactly? He wasn't sure. All he knew was that he suddenly felt empty inside. It wasn't at all how he expected to feel. It was a victory, after all. He'd won.

So then why did it feel like he was still missing something?

5:32 P.M.
FATHER KNOWS BEST

GAME OVER. THAT'S WHAT OZ HAD SAID. NO MORE messages. No bullies to beat. No races to run. No puzzles to solve. No rats or zombies or witches. Bryan could almost hear the end-credits music playing in the background, but he knew he was just imagining it.

As he walked, Bryan tried to recall everything that had happened, but some of the details were already blending together, parts of it so fantastic he was starting to wonder if he *hadn't* just made them up. Had there really been Russians humming while he was solving those geometry problems in Tennenbaum's class?

Did Mrs. Reynolds really bite Ms. Wang just to get a Twinkie? Was there ever a dragon in *Romeo and Juliet*? Maybe Bryan had imagined some of it. Maybe Myra was right and he was a paranormal schizofrenetic with an overactive imagination. A twelve-year-old kid working on six straight nights of playing the same stupid video game, hopped up on too much sugar and not enough sleep. The whole day was already hazing over, becoming hard to sort through, even harder to believe.

Even the fight with Wattly. It was real. Otherwise it wouldn't hurt to take a breath—but maybe it was *just* that. A stupid school-yard brawl—not some epic battle between good and evil. He hadn't slain some fiend from beyond the underworld. Wattly wasn't the devil. He was just a kid with a thick skull and parents who probably didn't hug him enough as a baby. Even the fight itself was a jumble in Bryan's head. A confusion of fists and feet and limbs and bodies with only the final image clear—of Tank balled up on the ground with his hands tucked between his legs. The rest was fuzzy. Pixilated. Like when you zoom in too close on a picture and lose sight of what you were looking at. The whole day was like that.

Except Jess. Her he could remember. The grass stains

on her elbows. The frayed ends of her shoelaces. The way she seemed to lean slightly sideways as she walked next to him. That sudden look of disappointment in her eyes when he mentioned Landon Prince, as if he'd given away the ending of some movie she'd been waiting to see.

Bryan stood at the end of his block. The white Civic was parked out front, which meant his dad had beaten him home. The very sight of his house with its overgrown hedges and cracked driveway—no coin slots—and the mat that said "Welcome" in twenty different languages, all too small to read, gave him some comfort. Tomorrow Bryan would wake up in this house, in the room looking out over the garage, and everything would be back to normal. His Boots of Average Walking Speed would just be tennis shoes. His alarm clock wouldn't ask him for a quarter. He wouldn't gain Fortitude when he ate his cereal and wouldn't lose hit points when he stubbed his toe. He would be back to his same old self. He hoped.

Bryan stood beside his father's car and checked his reflection in the driver's-side mirror, wiped off as much of the blood and dirt as he could manage, and adjusted his hair to hide the swelling on his forehead. He opened the front door slowly, hoping maybe to

JOHN DAVID ANDERSON

sneak by unnoticed. He got all the way to the landing before his father rounded the corner.

"You're home late."

Bryan stopped but didn't turn around.

"I was with Oz. Sorry. I should have called."

"Yeah, you should have," his father said. "But it's all right. Go wash up. Dinner's almost ready."

Back in his room with the door shut, Bryan tried turning his computer back on, but the machine was still fried. Beating up Chris Wattly hadn't brought it back to life. He took off his soiled shirt and changed into one featuring a band that was way too talented to be popular. He didn't bother to look at himself in the mirror. He knew he was a mess.

His father was already seated at the table when Bryan came down, the evening paper laid out beside his plate. Bryan sat and took a swallow of water, washing down the copper tang left from the blood on his lip, which stung against the cold glass. Suddenly, sitting there, he was overcome with exhaustion. And relief.

"Game's not over yet," his father muttered.

"What?" Bryan asked, sitting up, body suddenly stiff.

"Hmm?" his dad said, then pointed to the paper.

"Sorry. The series. Boston's up three to one, but I think Saint Louis can still come back. They just need more help from the bullpen." His father folded up the paper and pushed it aside, then looked across the table at Bryan, who tried to put his head down quickly, but not quickly enough. "What happened to your lip?" His father pointed his fork at Bryan's face.

"Dodgeball," Bryan said, picking the first thing that came to mind. Maybe not as good as *Fell off my bike*, but certainly better than *Got in a fistfight with a Tank*.

"That's one serious game of dodgeball," his father said with a whistle.

"Oh yeah," Bryan said.

"You know you are supposed to catch them with your hands, not with your mouth."

"I'll remember that for next time," Bryan said, though he hoped there wouldn't be a next time. Not like this time, anyway.

His father grunted, then took his fork and stabbed into his mashed potatoes with one hand. "So," he continued, "how was the rest of your day—outside of the dodgeball you tried to eat?"

Bryan moved the green beans around on his plate.

"Oh. You know. The usual. Quiz in math. Learned about mice in science. I got to be Romeo in English."

Bryan's dad smiled, put down his fork, and put up a hand in a dramatic pose. "'O Romeo, Romeo! Wherefore art thou Romeo?' That's pretty much the only part I remember," he admitted. Apparently, he'd never gotten to the part about the zombies. "It's a love story, you know," his father continued.

"Yeah, Dad. I think everybody pretty much knows that."

"But they're all love stories," his father mused. "All the good ones, anyway. Trouble is half of 'em are tragedies, too, so the guy never gets the girl. That's why the comedies are better. What's the point if you don't get the girl, you know what I mean?"

"Yeah, what's the point?" Bryan echoed.

He stabbed a bean and held it above the plate, just staring at it. What's the point? Oz had asked him sort of the same question when he said he wanted to unlock the secret level, back before this whole day even started. And Bryan had had to explain that it wasn't the end. Even after you beat the Demon King, there was still something more. There had to be.

Bryan looked across the table at his father. A professor of history at the local liberal arts college. He knew a whole lot of unimportant stuff—an encyclopedia of names and dates and other useless trivia. Most of the time, when Bryan wanted answers, he went to his mother—down-to-earth and logical. But this didn't strike Bryan as the kind of thing that logic had an answer for.

"Dad—did you ever have one of those days where you wake up and everything is just . . . different? Like you see the world differently? And everything you do is, like, I don't know . . . epic somehow . . . like it matters in a way that it doesn't normally?" Bryan paused. He wasn't sure he was explaining it well. Maybe there was no way to explain it, not without going into the details and sounding insane. But his father nodded anyway.

"Sure. I guess. I mean, most days are just *days*," he said. "Just like all the days before. But every now and then you come across a moment. That rare opportunity to do something that matters. Save the world or slay the giant or find the treasure, or, if you're really lucky, rescue the princess and ride off into the sunset," he said with a wink. "History is made of those days. They're the only ones worth remembering."

JOHN DAVID ANDERSON

"Wait, what was that last part again?" Bryan asked.

"What part? About history?"

But Bryan wasn't listening. He was looking out the window, at the dusky sky already marking the end of the day. He stood up and set his napkin next to his plate, all his food still untouched.

"Where are you going? You can't possibly be done."

"Exactly. I thought I was, but I was wrong. *So* wrong. I've got to go."

"What? You haven't even eaten anything!"

Bryan turned and grinned at his father. "There's no time. I know what I still have to do. Thanks, Dad. You're a genius."

He could hear his father still protesting, but he was already halfway to the stairs. There was no way he could explain, and even if he wanted to, there really wasn't time. The party started at seven, and it was already after six. As he took the stairs by twos, he heard his father calling out to him, "Do you want me to save it for later?"

"There are no saves," Bryan called back, then ducked into his room and pulled out his phone. He closed his door and sat in front of his dead computer, hands shaking. Oz picked up on the seventh ring.

"You still mad at me for getting kidnapped?"

"I was mad at you for getting me in trouble in the first place," Bryan said. "But not anymore. You still free tonight?"

"Seriously?"

"Seriously."

"Um. Let me check my schedule. Let's see . . . my dinner with the queen of England was canceled, so I guess, yeah, I'm not too busy."

"How soon can you get here?" Bryan asked, letting the sarcasm slide.

"Mom's asleep on the couch, and Dad's working late, so my sister would probably have to bring me. She's getting ready to go out with her girlfriends. She's still in the hair and makeup stage, so I'm thinking at least a half an hour."

"Do you think she would drop us off somewhere?"

"What do you mean, 'drop us off somewhere'? It's Friday night, man. *Game* night."

Bryan looked in the mirror this time, at the skinny kid with the flame-orange hair and the swollen lip. **GARB OF MINOR COOLNESS**, the label beside his clean shirt read.

"Exactly," Bryan said.

7:33 P.M.
THE WIZARD APPEARS

IT TOOK THE BETTER PART OF AN HOUR FOR OZ'S sister to put on her makeup. Bryan waited for them on the porch swing and texted Oz, informing him of what he was thinking and where they were headed. Oz texted back that he had already guessed where they were headed, he just wasn't sure *why*.

To rescue the princess, Bryan texted him.

He didn't get a response.

The cherry-red Guzman-family Grand Caravan pulled up into their drive fifteen minutes later. Oz's eighteen-year-old sister yelled through the passenger's-side window.

"I don't have any extra booster seats, so you'll have to grab one from your car."

She was funny that way. From inside the van he heard Oz tell her to shut up, starting a volley of "you shut ups" between them. Bryan zipped up his black hoodie and opened the passenger door. "Thanks, Carla," he said. "I appreciate it."

Oz's sister scowled at him and jerked her thumb backward.

"No one sits in front. I can't risk being seen with you guys." Bryan crawled into the back next to Oz. "Also no farting, fake farting, vomiting, fake vomiting, burping, or telling stupid jokes. I choose the radio station. And no comments about my singing. And use whispers when you talk so that your inane conversation doesn't drive me to cross over the median and kill us all. You buckled?"

Bryan nodded. Oz leaned close and whispered. "So it's *not* over?"

"It's not over."

Oz nodded thoughtfully, then reached into his pocket for his phone. "Oh, I almost forgot. I got this about fifteen minutes ago. It's a response to my

JOHN DAVID ANDERSON

message. The one I sent to the developers of Sovereign of Darkness? I'm afraid it's not much help."

Oz handed his phone to Bryan. The e-mail was short and polite, thanking them for being fans of the game and assuring them that they took all customer inquiries seriously.

It then went on to explain that there was absolutely no hidden level in Sovereign of Darkness, suggesting that maybe they had gotten their hands on a pirated copy or that someone had hacked into Bryan's computer and messed with the software somehow. It stated that any additional content they perceived as coming from the game was not licensed by the designers or the manufacturer and that GameThrottle Inc. could not be held liable for any consequences resulting from the play thereof.

It added that studies had shown that excessive video game playing had been known to cause or inadvertently contribute to a variety of physical symptoms, including eyestrain, carpal tunnel syndrome, muscle fatigue, stiffness, soreness, blurred vision, and, in very rare cases, seizures and heart attacks, and recommended that Bryan and Oz take frequent breaks in between gaming periods and to cease gaming altogether when such symptoms started to manifest themselves.

It concluded by thanking them again for their feedback and wishing them a happy resolution to their quest.

"So what does it mean?" Oz asked, taking his phone back.

Bryan shrugged. "It's basically telling us to get a life."

"Oh," Oz said, clearly daunted by the idea. "So what are you going to do if we get there and she's with Landon?"

"I don't know yet," Bryan said.

"What if Missy doesn't let us in?"

"I'm not sure."

"What if Tank and his buddies are there?"

Bryan hadn't thought about that. "I don't know, Oz. We'll figure it out."

Oz patted the pockets of his jacket and grinned. "It's all right," he said. "I've got you covered this time."

When they turned onto Missy's street, they could already hear shouting coming from her house. There were only four residences on the block, each with its own long, winding private driveway, each surrounded by a wrought-iron fence or high stone wall and an electronically sealed gate. Bryan was suddenly aware of how poorly dressed he was. His Breeches of Enduring Stiffness still had giant grass stains on them. His Boots of Average Walking Speed were caked in mud. He had, at least, thought to brush his hair.

"Jeez, what do you think one of these houses costs?" Oz said. "At least a million bucks?"

Carla stopped at the end of the street. She didn't even bother turning off the engine. "Call Mom when you are ready to be picked up. I'm not coming to get you. If you get in trouble, find a bus or have your new friend's chauffeur drive you home. I'm sure she has one, judging by the looks of this place."

Bryan thanked her again. She smiled at him, then rolled her eyes at Oz. "Now get out of my van."

"I hate sisters," he whispered as the van pulled away.

Bryan and Oz walked to the gate at the end of the Middletons' drive. It was at least ten feet tall and topped with black spikes. Bryan thought maybe he could get over it if he was careful, but he was sure Oz would skewer himself like a campfire marshmallow. So instead he pressed the button on the intercom. It was at least twenty seconds before anyone answered.

"Who is it?" It sounded like Missy's voice, or one of her clones'. Bryan thought about lying, using the name of one of the more popular kids, but he had no way of knowing who was already there and who wasn't. Besides, he shouldn't have to lie. He had been invited.

"Bryan Biggins," he said, then looked at Oz. "And guest."

He heard an audible groan through the speaker. Then some conversation. Someone laughed. There was another voice, a guy's voice saying, "Whatever." Then the intercom abruptly shut off.

"I don't think they're going to let us in, R2," Oz said, staring at the gate. "Should I try to call my sister and get her to turn around and come get us?" But before Oz could even get to his phone, the electronic latch on the gate released and it swung open, revealing a long, curving road leading up to Missy Middleton's mansion.

Bryan started up the driveway, Oz right beside him, looking even more out of place. He had at least thought to put on a jacket to cover the armpit stains. The party

JOHN DAVID ANDERSON

was in full swing. The air was crisp, the grass still damp. The temperature had dipped, but that didn't stop a few dozen Mount Comforters from congregating outside, cups and plates in hand, laughing and teasing, or pointing and looking disgusted. It was already dark out, which was good. Maybe he and Oz could just sneak in and find her without drawing too much attention to themselves. That's what Kerran Nightstalker would have done. Infiltration. Subterfuge. Stealth.

Except Bryan was no Kerran Nightstalker. This wasn't Sovereign of Darkness. Just one of those crazy, once-in-a-lifetime days where almost anything could happen.

"I don't think this is a good idea," Oz said, his hands tucked into his jacket pockets, nervously shuffling his feet up the blacktop.

"I have to do this," Bryan whispered. "If I don't do it today, I don't think I'll ever do it at all. And besides. You still owe me for saving your life." Oz didn't argue with that. He and Bryan made their way up the drive. Scattered across the lawn, the few groups of kids turned their heads and stared. Bryan could feel their eyes. He looked around for Jess, but he knew he wouldn't find her. She was here—he was certain of it. But she was inside the house that looked almost like a castle, or big enough to be one, at least.

They made it halfway to the house before they were stopped.

It was Zach Rollins, from the baseball diamond, and three of his buddies, standing shoulder to shoulder. A wall of muscle, blocking the way.

"That's far enough, Bryan," Zach said.

They actually used his real name, Bryan thought. That was a first.

"I'm just here to see Jess. Then I'll leave. I promise."

The four boys looked at one another, then back at Bryan. He could feel Oz tensing beside him. The gate at the bottom of the drive was already shut and locked again.

"Who says she wants to see you?" Zach said.

"I just want to talk to her. Five minutes." Zach had his thick brown arms crossed, but Bryan noticed none of the four boys moved any closer. Surely, they weren't scared of him. "If you want me to leave, you're going to have to throw me out," Bryan said. Oz glanced at him with a worried expression.

"We can probably manage that," Zach said, then nodded to his friends, the cue for all four of them to advance, spreading out so that they could get on both sides.

Oz leaned in close and whispered in Bryan's ear: "Told you, man. I've got this."

"Oz?" Bryan hissed back in warning. "Whatever you are about to do—" He didn't get a chance to finish the thought.

"You might want to stand back," Oz interrupted, then he suddenly leaped forward, pulling both hands out of his jacket pockets. Each of them held a small black device, slightly curved, with metal prongs—like rounded fangs—jutting out from the end. Bryan had seen enough action movies to know what they were.

"Do *not* take another step!" Oz bellowed.

Zach and his friends froze.

"*What*," Bryan whispered, taking a step away from Oz as well, "are you doing with *those*?"

"They're my mom's," Oz said out of the corner of his mouth, clutching a stun gun in each hand. "She's deathly afraid of parking lots at night. She keeps one in the car and another in her purse. Now listen, when

I charge, you break for the house. Got it?"

"What do you mean, when you charge?" Bryan said through clenched teeth, glancing nervously at Rollins and his posse, then back to the stun guns in Oz's hands, but his best friend ignored him. Oz raised both hands high into the air, and suddenly two arcs of blue electricity erupted from them, piercing the evening sky, illuminating Oz's wide, wild eyes.

"Behold," he boomed. "It is I! Oz, the great and terrible! Tremble at my power and kneel before me!" His voice carried across the lawn, getting the attention of almost everyone outside. Bryan stared for a moment at his friend, silhouetted against the night sky, face bathed in the blue glow of the electric arcs that crackled from his fingertips.

Then Oz charged the group of boys, the stun guns still sparking and zapping from both fists like cracked lightning. Zach Rollins grabbed the shirt of one of his friends and spun him around, all four of them scattering as Oz chased after them, letting out a war cry.

"I said 'tremble'!"

Bryan stood stupefied and watched the Wizard of Elmhurst Park amble across the lawn, electricity dancing in his palms, scattering the crowd like a charging rhino escaped from the zoo. He considered chasing after him, afraid he might electrocute someone—himself, most likely—but then he looked at the house again.

She was in there somewhere. Waiting for him.

"Thanks, Oz," Bryan whispered, then ran up the rest of the drive to the house. He paused at the door for a moment, feeling in his jeans pocket.

He still had one continue left.

8:16 P.M.
THE FINAL CONFRONTATION

↓

THERE WERE BODIES EVERYWHERE. FURNITURE— expensive and uncomfortable-looking—had been pushed aside to make room to dance on the hardwood floors, though nobody bothered. Instead they stood around, stuffing their faces and shouting at one another to be heard over the boppy pop music that pulsed out of Missy Middleton's speakers. The whole place reeked of queso and body spray. Bryan wasn't a huge fan of either. He felt completely out of place.

He pushed his way into the crowd and was immediately jostled aside, nearly falling into a potted cactus that stood guard by the front door. He scanned the room, but it was impossible to pick out a single face from the herd, even a face as unforgettable as Jessica Alcorn's. She had to be here somewhere. He felt a tap on his shoulder.

"How did *you* get in here?"

It was the host of the party. The keeper of the castle. Wearing too much makeup and not enough fabric to cover half of her body, hair held chemically in place. Apparently, she had not approved the opening of the gate. She scowled at Bryan through her glittery lip gloss. Not that he cared. Maybe this morning it would have mattered what Missy Middleton thought of him, but not so much anymore.

"Where's Jess?" he asked.

"Ex*cuse* me?" Missy said.

"I said, where . . . is . . . Jess?" Bryan repeated, shouting to be heard over the din. "I need to talk to her."

Missy didn't say a word, but her eyes flashed to the long, winding staircase at the back of the room. Bryan turned to go but felt Missy's claw digging into his arm.

"Don't you *dare* go up there!" she screeched, grabbing hold with her other talon, but at that same moment someone stuffed his head in the front door and yelled something about a lunatic running around on the lawn with a stun gun, claiming to be the reincarnation of Thor.

Oz. The god of thunder. Coming to the rescue again.

The sudden outflow of bodies wanting to go and see was more than enough distraction for Bryan to pull away from Missy and make his way toward the stairs, except now he was working against the tide, a horde of kids threatening to trample him, spilling the contents of their cups on his shoes, driving him backward. He leaped onto a couch to get clear of the crowd, nearly slamming his head against a low-hanging chandelier. He jumped to a leather recliner and then to a coffee table covered with magazines—*Boating World* and *Food & Wine*—feet sliding on their slick covers, nearly losing his balance and falling into the pack. He didn't see any way to get across the sea of bodies. He was about to just dive into the crowd when a girl he didn't recognize yelled that she had dropped her phone, and three people bent over to try and find it, falling to their hands and knees, creating a path of arched backs leading straight to the staircase. He only needed to hop across without falling.

Easier than crossing the street after school, at least, Bryan thought, and leaped from the coffee table onto

JOHN DAVID ANDERSON

the back of the first girl, then one-footed it from back to back, ignoring the shouts of the people he stepped on, and used the cushion of an ottoman as a trampoline to leap up and grab hold of the banister. One hand slipped, too sweaty, but he held on with the other. With a grunt he hauled himself over and onto the staircase, thanking Mr. Gladspell for making him do pull-ups in gym class. He'd made it across. He climbed to a group of kids milling on the landing at the top.

"Jess Alcorn?"

A boy pointed to the door at the end of the hall. "Balcony, I think."

Balcony.

Where else?

Bryan pushed past another gaggle of Mount Comfort students waddling down the hall to see what the commotion was about, and squeezed through the door and into an empty room that looked like an office, with a roll-top desk and dusty shelves. On the far side was a sliding glass door leading out to the balcony that wrapped halfway around Missy Middleton's second story, overlooking her backyard and the guesthouse, where, supposedly, her parents were bunkered, hopefully oblivious to what

INSERT COIN TO CONTINUE

was going on outside. He worried for Oz, but there was nothing he could do about that now except not waste the moment he'd been given.

Bryan hesitated at the door, though, legs locked, hands shaking. He could see the full moon through the glass, as well as his own reflection in it. The bump on his forehead was clearly visible now. There was a crack in his bottom lip. Mud on his pants. Dark rings around his eyes. He was a wreck. He couldn't go out and talk to her looking like this, could he?

Then, suddenly, inexplicably, Bryan became gorgeous. Staring at his shimmering image in the glass door, he transformed into someone tall and handsome, with snow-white teeth and perfect hair, a silk complexion and beaming, bright eyes. Bryan blinked once, mesmerized, thinking of fairy godmothers and magic wands, before he realized what he was looking at.

The door slid open and Landon Prince stood there, chin to nose with Bryan.

He didn't look too happy.

"Biggins," he said, sounding not at all surprised. Bryan took a step back.

"Prince," he murmured.

Downstairs the music suddenly shifted, the party pop fading out, replaced with the singular heartbeat of a bass line that Bryan could feel pulsing through the floorboards. Landon Prince stood in the door, blocking the way, his letter jacket draped over his shoulder. One final obstacle. Bryan tensed, eyes narrowing. His heartbeat slammed against his chest. He waited for the walls to shake and the floor to split beneath them. He waited for the overhead lamp to explode in a shower of sparks. He waited for the tumbleweed to come bouncing along the carpet. He could see it all so clearly in his head. He knew what had to happen now.

Prince drew his sword and pointed it at Bryan's chest. "En garde," he said.

Or maybe . . .

Prince's right hand dropped to the revolver at his side. "This balcony's not big enough for the both of us," he said.

Or possibly . . .

Prince's muscles bulged, tearing through his shirt, buttons pinging off the walls, as his body grew to twice its normal size and turned a sickly green, the color of pureed peas. "Grawrarrr," he said.

INSERT COIN TO CONTINUE

Even . . .

Prince's face melted, revealing the red leather skin and curved black horns of the Demon King beneath. "Wattly," he said.

Bryan shook his head, clearing the images that had piled up there. "Huh?"

Landon Prince pointed at Bryan's face. "Wattly," he repeated. "Did he do that?" He was pointing to the scrapes and bruises and bumps.

Honestly, Bryan couldn't remember. He self-consciously sucked on his split lower lip. "Mostly," he said. He was still waiting for Landon's face to melt. It wasn't melting. It was just as handsome as ever. Landon Prince shook his head.

"I heard you laid him out pretty good, though. He was asking for it. The guy's kind of a jerk." Landon paused, glanced behind him. "I suppose you're look-ing for Jess."

Bryan nodded.

Landon nodded.

They both just stood there in the awkward silence, nodding at each other. Maybe there wasn't going to be a sword fight, but wasn't Landon going to push him, at least? Tell him to bug off? Call him names? Grab him by his shirt and throw him off the balcony? Bryan had been prepared for any of these—save maybe the being thrown off the balcony part. He wasn't prepared for this, though. He wasn't ready for *nothing* to happen. He wasn't ready for Landon just to let him go.

Maybe Oz was right. Everybody thinks everybody is out to get them, but that's not true. Sometimes a Prince is just a Prince.

Landon ran a fork of fingers through his hair, which fell right back into place, unmussed, then stepped past Bryan without a shoulder shove or a hip check or even a word. No headlocks. No body slams. No challenge. Bryan turned and watched him head for the hallway, waiting for the sneak attack, but Landon simply paused in the doorframe and looked back at Bryan standing by the sliding glass with the dark sky beyond.

"She talks about you sometimes, you know," he said; then he vanished down the hall.

Bryan stared at the empty space he'd left for a while. *She talks about me?* he thought.

He turned back to the balcony. With one hand in his pocket he stepped through.

INSERT COIN TO CONTINUE

8:23 P.M.
THE LAST COIN

SHE STOOD ALONE—AT LAST ALONE—WEARING A new pair of jeans and one of those shirts that made one think of pirates or peasants, Bryan wasn't sure which, frilly and billowy and embroidered along the sleeves. She was staring out over the backyard, down at the lights reflected in the swimming pool that hadn't been covered yet, spotted with leaves that gathered in clumps by the edges. Rows of pale-pink rosebushes lined the fence. Out in the front yard Oz was probably still pretending to shoot bolts of lightning from his fingertips, but here in the back it was peaceful, picturesque, like something from the cover of a magazine.

The cute girl you're smitten with stands up on the balcony, bathed in moonlight.

Bryan couldn't remember his line. Something about softly breaking a window. He would need to improvise. He felt in his pocket for his last coin. His last continue. He cleared his throat and held it up where she could see it.

"Penny for your thoughts."

Jess turned abruptly, eyes squinting, skeptical, as if she didn't believe what she was seeing, as if maybe Bryan was just a figment of her imagination. "What are you doing here?"

She didn't sound angry or defensive or even surprised. She sounded curious, as if she had an answer in mind and wanted to see if he could guess it. "You invited me," he said.

"I thought you had baseball practice?"

"Canceled," Bryan said. On account of it not really existing in the first place. "I might have made it up," he confessed. "Because I'm kind of an idiot. And I was nervous. I don't get invited to a lot of these." He stretched his arms to indicate the house, the party, all of it.

"I see you got over it, though," she prodded.

"I had to work my way up to it," Bryan said. *Believe me.* He took a deep breath and stepped farther out onto the balcony and up to the railing, so that he was directly across from her, now only a few feet away. Missy Middleton's backyard was a carefully sculpted paradise—stone benches and a vine-covered gazebo and several gardens in various stages of blossom and shed, nothing like his little patch of green at home with its one tire swing and overgrown ivy.

"It's really pretty up here." He avoided looking at her when he said it—in case she got the right idea.

"It's perfect," she replied. "If you like that sort of thing." That same frustrating strand of black hair had come loose again, but she didn't bother to tuck it away this time. She looked at him sideways along the ledge, leaning on her elbows, the moonlight catching half of her face. Suddenly she looked concerned. Beautiful but concerned. She was looking at the bruise on his forehead. "Is that from this afternoon?" Jess reached over and touched it gingerly with the tip of one finger, just barely, but Bryan still felt a kind of electric shock. "Does it hurt?" she asked.

Bryan tried not to wince. "Not really," he lied. "I mean, yeah. Kind of. A lot. When you touch it."

Jess jerked her hand back.

"No. I'm kidding. It's all right," he said. "I'm all right. It's not that bad."

"It was stupid," she said. "I can't believe you even did that."

Did that. She meant got in a fight with Wattly, but the same could have been said for half a dozen things Bryan had done today, most of which he could barely believe himself. "I know," he said. "I figured that's why you asked me to walk you home this afternoon. You know—to get me out of it." It hadn't worked, of course, but that was hardly her fault.

"That's not why I asked," she said. "I just wanted you to walk me home."

Bryan risked looking her in the eyes, the same color as half the leaves drifting lazily to the grass below. Jess, who remembered about the sandwich. Who talked about him sometimes. Who didn't like things perfect— thank God. She'd wanted him to walk her home. Him.

From around the front of the house, Bryan thought he could hear shouting, but Jess didn't seem to notice, or if she did, she didn't care. She was looking back at Bryan, daring him, it seemed, to speak. There was no turning back now.

"I'm going to say something, and it's probably going to sound stupid or lame, but just let me get it out and try not to laugh, okay?"

Jess nodded, not taking her eyes off of him. He thought about everything he'd been through today, everything he'd done. This, by far, was the hardest. He took a deep breath.

Jess Alcorn—I have battled witches and Tanks. I have stolen treasure and fought in wars and solved equations and nearly been run over, twice. I have faced spiders and mice and Bosses and Princes. I have been beaten, again and again, but I've continued and continued and continued. And now, finally, I'm here. Finally I think I can say what I've wanted to say for years.

Bryan set the penny on the ledge between them.

"This has probably been the absolute worst day of my life," he said, breathless. "But right now . . . at this moment . . . it's totally worth it."

Jess shook her head, but she didn't laugh.

"You're kinda weird. You know that, right?" she asked.

Bryan nodded. It was hard to argue, but it wasn't exactly the response he was hoping for.

Before he could say anything else, though, Jess smiled. "But you're pretty sweet, too." She looked up at the moon, then reached for the penny on the ledge, balancing it carefully on her thumbnail. "Make a wish," she said.

"Me?"

"It's your penny," she said.

So Bryan shut his eyes; he made a wish, then he opened them just as Jess flicked the penny into the night. He watched it, his last coin, pirouette up over the ledge, heads over tails, glinting once, like a firefly, before disappearing into the electric-blue water of the pool below. Then Jess turned so that their noses were almost touching, and he could feel her breath on his cheek.

"So this is how it ends," he said.

"Maybe not," she said with a shrug.

Bryan Biggins closed his eyes.

He never saw the writing in the sky.

He didn't need to.

SATURDAY
THE DAY AFTER FRIDAY

BRYAN BIGGINS SAT UP WITH A START.

Somehow he had slept through his alarm. He looked at the clock sitting by his bed. It was already 9:38. He had overslept. He was late for school. Forget being late for Mr. Tennenbaum's class again. He had slept through math entirely.

Then it hit him: It was Saturday. His parents had let him sleep in. He had dropped off the moment his body hit the sheets and hadn't moved.

And he had been having the strangest dream.

Bryan rubbed his eyes and stretched his legs,

swinging them easily out of bed. He was still dressed in last night's clothes. The filthy jeans. The sweaty T-shirt. He put his head in his hands, trying to sift through the muddled fog in his brain, trying to remember everything that had happened, to separate what was real from what wasn't, when something on his nightstand began to buzz. He panicked, one hand instinctively reaching for his pocket, for a nickel or dime, and finding it empty. Then he relaxed.

It was only his phone. He had two new text messages already this morning. The first was a long one from Oz, saying that he would have to cancel Saturday-night game night and the next ten game nights on account of being grounded for stealing his mom's stun guns and getting chased off private property, but that it was worth it just to see the looks on everyone's faces last night. He asked Bryan to call him as soon as he got the chance because they had a lot to talk about.

The second was from her.

Free this afternoon? Wanna hang out at the park? Sandwiches. No mustard. Y/N?

Bryan smiled a cracked and swollen smile.

The girl you like asks you if you want to hang out at the park. Yes or no. Press any key to continue.

Bryan took a deep breath, finger poised over his phone.

He had never been 100 percent completely sure of anything in his life.

Until now.

JOHN DAVID ANDERSON

EPILOGUE:
DEFEATING THE DEMON KING . . .
AGAIN. AGAIN.

*"GREETINGS, CHOSEN ONE. I HAVE BEEN EXPECT-*ing you."

"Oh, you have, have you?"

"Welcome to my lair."

"Seen it all before, jerkwad."

"I had hoped you would join me, but now I see that your heart is impure. I have no choice but to destroy you."

"Right. Like to see you try."

"Then let us begin, warrior, so I can wallow in a bath of your cruor."

"Oh yeah. Bring it. Taste that. Hmm? You like that? Want a little more? Oh, really? You're off to see the wizard now, baby. You thought my buddy Bryan was tough? Wait till you see what I got planned for you. You think that's going to work? Chew on this. . . . Oh yeah. See that? Here it comes. HERE . . . IT . . . COMES. And *skadabam*!"

"NOOOOOOOOOOOOOOOO!!!"

"Yeah! Take that, you exploding chunk monkey. That's right. Who da man? Who da MAN? Who da . . . what the *heck*?"

Oswaldo froze in his chair and stared dumbly at the screen as the pieces of the Demon King reassembled themselves before his very eyes.

"*Congratulations, warrior. It is time for your true journey to begin.*"

ACKNOWLEDGMENTS

This book is dedicated to fun. No doubt I will hear about this from my wife, children, and/or mother, but I dedicated the book to the very thing it was written for. Writing *Insert Coin to Continue* was a romp. It made me feel like I was twelve again, but not in a here-comes-the-acne-and-awkwardness way. In a good way. In a did-you-know-there-was-a-secret-code-that-gives-you-infinite-lives kind of way. In a first kiss kind of way.

And there are a lot of people I have to thank for making it such a blast to write.

First off—big thanks to Amy Cloud, my editor, who sounds like she should be the protagonist in a kick-butt RPG. Thank you for your unending patience, wisdom, and enthusiasm, and for helping this book reach the next level without making me start over. You are the Clank to my Ratchet. The power pellet to my Pacman. The Luigi to my Mar . . . you know what . . . I'll just stop there.

To the rest of the team at Aladdin—Mandy Veloso, Erica Stahler, and Karin Paprocki—many thanks for correcting my math and for whipping *Coin* into shape.

I couldn't have asked for a better squad. Thanks also to Orlando Arocena for making the little boy inside me pine for the days of dropping quarters into Galaga every time I look at this awesome cover.

Thanks to Adams Literary for their persistence, finding a home for all of my stories, even the whacky ones. I'm going to try and get you guys to publish my collection of limericks from the second grade next.

To my family and friends for their continued support—to my lovely wife, Alithea, and especially to my kids, Nick and Isabella, who are in many ways responsible for this book. Life is a crazy game. There are a lot of levels to gain, a lot of puzzles to solve, a lot of bosses to beat, but you have taught me to have fun playing and never give up.

Because the rewards are worth unlocking.

ABOUT THE AUTHOR

JOHN DAVID ANDERSON writes novels for young people and then, occasionally, gets them published. He is the author of *Posted*, *Ms. Bixby's Last Day*, *Sidekicked*, *Standard Hero Behavior*, *Minion*, and *The Dungeoneers*. He lives with his patient wife and brilliant twins in Indianapolis, Indiana, right next to a state park and a Walmart. He enjoys hiking, reading, chocolate, spending time with his family, playing the piano, chocolate, not putting away his laundry, watching movies, and chocolate. He likes video games where mustachioed plumbers fall into pools of lava and thinks twenty minutes of Dance Dance Revolution counts as a full cardio workout. He has leveled up forty-one times, but he hasn't grown up yet.